Cassie

AFTER
ANTIETAM

Other books by Myrtle Long Haldeman:
  Cassie: The Girl With the Hero's Heart

  To order, call 1-800-765-6955.

  Visit us at www.reviewandherald.com for information on other Review and Herald® products.

MYRTLE LONG HALDEMAN

Cassie

AFTER
ANTIETAM

REVIEW AND HERALD® PUBLISHING ASSOCIATION
HAGERSTOWN, MD 21740

This book was
Edited by Delma Miller
Cover design/art direction by O'Connor Creative
Digital photo illustration by Lyn Boyer
Digital photography by Joel D. Springer
Typeset: 12/15 Bembo

PRINTED IN U.S.A.

08 07 06 05 04   5 4 3 2 1

R&H Cataloging Service
Haldeman, Myrtle Long, 1924–
    Cassie after Antietam.

    I. Title.

            813.54

ISBN 0-8280-1782-4

Dedication

To my three youngest, beloved grandchildren,
sons of Daniel and Patricia Wise.

Nathaniel (Nat) Wise (age 4)
Theodore (Teddy) Wise (age 2)
Christian (Kit) Wise (almost 1)

That they and their peers may learn about life
as it was lived more than 140 years before
their time, about the aftermath of war and
how our ancestors survived it,
and about growing strong through suffering.

Acknowledgments

As I read books about the reconstruction period after the Civil War, I felt an urge to write about life during that time and to continue my family's saga. (My grandfather and Cassie's father, David Long, were brothers.) As in my first book, *Cassie, the Girl With a Hero's Heart,* the story line is realistic but fictionalized.

Thanks to the persistent research of Omer M. Long, much of my data was found in the genealogy, *The Descendents of Isaac Long,* compiled by Omer M. Long.

My two brothers, Joseph and John Long, kindly supplied details of rural life which were pertinent to the story. Others assisting in research included the following:

Ted Camp, St. James School
Brian Moore, pastor, St. James Brethren Church
John Frye, Washington County Library
Lou Kensinger, Martinsburg, Pennsylvania
Staff members at Washington County Historical Society

Many thanks to each of these!

Two books of particular help were:
Freeman Ankrum's *Sidelights on Brethren History,* and John W. Schildt's *Drums Along the Antietam.*

Chapter 1

It was late fall in 1862. Although the Antietam battle was over, Federal troops were encamped from Harpers Ferry, West Virginia, to Hancock, Maryland. Many camped on the farms near Sharpsburg, Maryland, pillaging the owners' cornfields and tons of hay to feed their horses. Bushels of potatoes were roasted over campfires to feed half-starved and wounded soldiers.

As Cassie and Mandy took a break from chores, they surveyed the ravaged farm that was their home. Sitting under a big oak tree on the front lawn, they quietly

The David Long home. Situated on about 200 acres of land, the home was like the average home of that day, built to accommodate both family and guests amply. The church met there for a time. During the Battle of Antietam this house was within range of both armies. The soldiers tramped over the farm, damaging it as they went. Little damage was done to the house, although a cannonball penetrated the east wall.

viewed the wreckage. The worm fence that once bordered their lane and enclosed their fields was now a shambles. Some panels were still intact, while other rails were broken or totally missing. Only the two rows of big oak trees now defined the roadway.

They watched the few chickens making footprints in the dirt as they scratched primly for tasty worms and bugs. Hens clucked happily as the girls clucked back and tossed them occasional crumbs from their dress pockets.

"I heard a rooster crow early this morning," said Mandy. "I hope he sees we get some baby chicks in the spring. Soldiers didn't leave many for us. We be poor on chicken and eggs this winter."

"Yes, I wonder how we're all going to have enough to eat," replied Cassie. "We need at least three hogs to supply us with meat. We'll need to keep a mama hog to have babies next year. We'll be short on milk, too, since some of our cows took off cross-country when they found the fences wide open. I hope they find their way home again. I miss Old Bossy. She gave us big buckets of milk."

A cottontail scuttled through the grass; then sat motionless, its big dark eyes intent on the two friends.

Mandy laughed. "What he think he is, comin' so close? Guess the dogs haven't seen him or he'd be hoppin' fast as lightnin'. We'll be havin' him for supper real soon!"

Cassie felt something brush her ankle. She looked down and saw their dog, Jack, wagging his tail.

"Oh, Jack wants to be petted. He's so proud of chasing that deer out of the garden. The deer will really keep him chasin'—we'll be having deer steaks on our table this fall. They'll take the place of other meat."

Mandy petted Jack happily and laid her head against his long silky hair. Feeling his reward, Jack soon crept quietly under the porch to rest in its cool shade.

The screen door on the porch opened as Mother called, "Girls, you've had a nice rest. Now it's time to come in and do some cleanup for Sunday."

Reluctantly Cassie and Mandy left their shaded retreat and strolled slowly toward the house.

"I was hoping Ella and Susan had finished that job by now," said Cassie. "Work never stops. I guess we're lucky to be younger. I know we don't work as hard as they do. When they get married, then we'll get all the hard work."

"Don't want to think 'bout that," answered Mandy. "Guess we better enjoy playtime when we can."

The girls hurried to their sweeping, dusting, and scrubbing, eager to see the end of it.

"You did well, girls," said Mother. "Now we'll have to think about supper. There's still some carrots and squash left in the garden. We'll roast some sweet potatoes in the fireplace ashes. Melvin and Joseph went fishing—I'm counting on some fresh fish for supper. We can take some dried apples out of the jar in the cupboard and cook them in a syrup of wild honey. With a bit of cream, they'll be a tasty treat for all of us."

"Oh, I can't wait for supper," exclaimed Mandy. "Sounds delicious!"

Off they dashed to the garden to gather some vegetables. Inside, Ella and Susan busily prepared the sweet potatoes for roasting and put the apples to soak. Fannie decided to add hot biscuits to round out the meal. She set to work eagerly, anticipating the wonderful aroma and mouthwatering taste of biscuits straight from the oven.

Later, when the men strode into the kitchen, faces glistening with sweat, they washed up, satisfied that the day's work was accomplished.

Quickly family members took their seats around the long table. Quiet reigned as they bowed their heads for the ritual blessing. Each one waited patiently as the food was passed down the line around the table. Hearty eaters, they soon emptied the dishes and left not a morsel on their plates.

Father pushed back his chair, and with eyes blue and merry, began a story:

> "As I was going to St. Ives
> I met a man with seven wives.
> Each wife had seven sacks,
> Each sack had seven cats,
> Each cat had seven kits.
> Kits, cats, sacks, and wives,
> How many were going to St. Ives?"

The silence was complete as each one tested his/her mental arithmetic. Suddenly, Melvin's hand shot up! "One person was going to St. Ives—all the others were what he saw."

"You're right, my son," said Father. "You've a quick mind. Now we must get on with our work plans. You all know that Sam Mumma's farm went up in smoke. He lost about everything he owned. Between the Union and Confederate armies, he lost furniture, clothing, grain, the whole corn crop, hay, and farm implements. When we talked, he said, 'The next time they fight, I hope they will get out of my cornfields. We have no corn or crops this year.'

"Our church brothers and other neighbors are planning a barn raisin' starting Monday. Many hands make light work, so if we have a good turnout, it won't take many days to see a new barn over there. We'll have to stick together and help each other. We're all short of food for the winter, but we believe the Lord will provide."

Father continued, "It seems the Antietam battle closed the door forever on a divided nation. After the rebels withdrew, England and France decided not to enter the war on the side of the South. Millions of Europeans had

Cassie's father, David Long, was a prominent elder of the German Baptist Brethren church in Middle Marland. A man of great generosity, he once attended a slave sale, purchased all the slaves, and set them free. He preached the last sermon on the second Sunday in September 1863 in the Mumma church before the bloody Battle of Antietam. More than 100 people flocked to his home that afternoon and evening as the armies took up their position on the ridge beyond his home.

no understanding of representative government. The door was closed on slavery with President Lincoln's Emancipation Proclamation.

"Instead, the door opened to caring for the wounded. It was the beginning of a new birth of freedom and a new America. The whole area between Boonsboro and Sharpsburg is one vast hospital. Houses and barns are filled with the wounded. Nearly everybody roundabout is engaged in waiting on and ministering to their needs."

"Yes," said Mother Mary, "in Hagerstown, the Ladies' Union Relief Association has been at work night and day. At night they meet in homes to sew bandages and make other things to relieve suffering. All day they're in the hospitals or out in the towns searching for, begging, or buying such articles as the sufferers want. On all the streets you see them with husbands, children, and servants carrying baskets, buckets, pitchers, and plates filled with delicate morsels. Many an unfortunate fellow weeps tears of joy as their gentle and kind words invite him to partake of the refreshing food."

Hers was a gentle reminder that the Long family was not alone in their acts of charity and helpfulness.

Again Father spoke: "Another thing we need to discuss is butchering day. Those hogs have fattened nicely, and the weather is getting frosty. Probably after we get Sam's barn up, we should get to butchering those hogs—like a week from Monday, if the day's cold enough."

All nodded their assent, as they anticipated the wonderful aroma of fresh pork roasting and the smoking of hams.

TWO WEEKS LATER

"Looks like tomorrow will be a good butchering day—it's turning colder. Boys, we'll need to set up everything today so's we can get an early start. Girls, you can get things set up in the washhouse—wood for the fire, all the buckets, tubs, basins, and kettles clean and ready to go," instructed Father.

Next morning all were up before dawn. Breakfast and morning prayers over, they headed out to their assigned tasks. Melvin first removed the gun from over the door.

As Cassie and Mandy gazed at the sky, they saw the sun burst on their world and felt the dawn's dewy freshness. It was breathtaking! It felt great to be alive! Roosters greeted the dawn with their raucous crowing. This gave the family added incentives to get moving on their assigned tasks.

Julia and Victor followed the menfolk so they could be near the exciting events. The barn was the scene of the main happening. One by one the hogs were corralled. With his gun Melvin sighted his target and pulled the trigger. His aim was true, so each animal died quickly. The sounds of the shots were no longer frightening, even to the little ones. It was nothing after so recently hearing the noise of battle.

A barrel of boiling water was standing by for the next step. The hog was lifted by block and tackle above the barrel and released gradually until the body was completely submerged. Soon the hog was lifted from the barrel and strung up for scraping. Circular metal scrapers with sharp edges and wooden handles were applied to the hog's skin. To speed the process, several of the girls helped Melvin and Joseph. All hair must be removed from head to feet, since all the meat was usable. Next came a complete washdown of the body. It must be thoroughly clean for cooking. The men then split the underside open with sharp knives. They removed all the insides, with usable parts going into one tub and waste into another.

Temporary tables had been set up with trestles and boards. The men placed each half on the table for cutting up—into hams, shoulders, sidemeat, and spareribs. Mother Mary emptied the stomach and, stretching it out on a board, scraped the inside lining free to prepare it for stuffing. It was a favorite meal in the Long household—hog maw stuffed with potatoes, sausage, onions, and bread stuffing. Baked in its juices, it was mouthwaterin' good! Head meat and organs were cooked to be ground into puddin'. Corn cakes and puddin'—what a great breakfast that would be!

The pig tail was a source of great fun for Cassie and Mandy. They took turns finding a likely victim, then pinning the tail on an appropriate spot of clothing (in the back) without the person's realizing it. First it was Fannie. The two girls were convulsed with giggles when Fannie discovered it and tried to unpin it. Pinned through several layers of cloth, it took some doing to remove it. She angrily threw it on the ground away from her, then glared at the two culprits.

"That was really mean," she scolded. "You need some work to do!"

"Mother," she called, "you'd better put these two at the sausage stuffer—that might keep them out of trouble."

Cassie and Mandy had already disappeared and were heading for another victim.

One plaything from the butchering was the bladder, blown up into a balloon and tied tightly with a string. Julia and Victor threw it into the air and batted it back and forth or used it to play kickball. Sometimes Joseph joined them in the game.

After Cassie and Mandy tired of their pig tail game, they took it to the fireplace to roast over the hot coals, where it sizzled and fried. When nicely browned, it became a delectable snack.

Mother Mary and Mama Sally were busy in the kitchen roasting chunks of meat in the oven and storing it in crocks with hot lard poured over. It would keep well in the cellar for use in the winter. Hams and shoulders were covered with a mixture of salt, saltpeter, and pepper. The smokehouse was a small building where an open fire of hickory chips could be built that would produce continual quantities of smoke. After the hams hung in the smoke for a number of days, they were ready to wrap in paper and hang in the attic for the winter.

It was an exhausting day! The noon meal served as a break from their arduous tasks, as well as an immediate reward for their efforts. A hearty feast of spareribs, mashed potatoes, sauerkraut, homemade bread, and green beans, followed by peach and apple pies, was a pleasant respite.

In the afternoon the work continued until all the necessaries were completed. After a simple supper, the family gathered for their evening worship—tired but happy with a job well done.

Chapter 2

Fall found the Long household in a whirlwind of busyness. Any produce still remaining in the kitchen garden needed to be rescued before the first hard frost would render it useless. Potatoes, carrots, cabbages, beets, squash of all colors—green, orange, yellow—and pumpkins, too, were carried into the cellar for storage. With the slanted outside cellar doors open to steps leading into the cellar, the task was made easier. While the supply was less than half the usual, that made each item more precious, and soon the garden was stripped of vegetables.

Six daughters of David and Mary Reichard Long. They had 12 children, 11 of whom grew to adulthood. Three of their daughters married ministers, and four of their five sons became ministers. From my research, here's who I think they are: (standing, left to right) Julie, Fannie, Cassie, and Susan; (seated) Ella and Lizzie.

The girls chatted together happily as they wove onions into long ropes or strung red and green peppers onto long strings. Merrily they carried their finished projects to the attic for drying. Moisture-free was a necessity for successful drying, and the heat of the attic guaranteed that.

Mother Mary was not far behind. She had been collecting her spicy herbs for cooking and her bitter herbs for medicine. Tying them in bundles, she added them to the offerings in the attic.

Another chore for Cassie and Mandy was to gather rags for stuffing cracks in the window frames. Upstairs and downstairs they went from room to room, stuffing bits and pieces of rags into cracks to keep out the cold air of winter. When the winter wind whistled outside, the family would be snug from the blasts of cold air.

Outside, the menfolk gathered traps from the shed to bring inside to grease at night by the warm fire. There was wildlife in abundance to supplement the winter food supply. Muskrats and mink were plentiful by the creek. Middle-sized traps were set for foxes in the woods. Father had taught Melvin and Joseph the process of skinning the animals and preparing the hides to sell. It would be a good source of income in the lean months.

Deer and rabbits startled easily and moved swiftly. Hunting was a way of thinning out wildlife that was so destructive to crops. Then, too, the added meat could replace the usual supply already consumed by soldiers. The menfolk salted and stretched the deerskins to make leather for shoes.

On the warmer days Melvin and Joseph could guiltlessly escape their farm chores. A string of fish, cleaned and salted down in barrels, would be a welcome addition to any meal.

Winter came in with a vengeance! The wind howled outside with a cold and friendless sound. At the Long home a giant limb from the oak tree cracked off during the high wind. When it fell against the frozen earth, it made an earsplitting crash, creating a fright within the household. The subzero temperatures turned the waters of the streams into frozen waterways. Antietam Creek boasted a thickness of 12 inches of ice and on the Potomac River ice measured 18 to 20 inches thick. Melvin reported that neighbor Miller hauled sycamore logs on a sled pulled by six horses down the frozen creek to the sawmill.

As darkness crept in early, the cold tightened around the house, when even the rags in the window cracks couldn't keep out all the biting air.

At night the family snuggled into their cornstalk beds and pulled up their feather tick covers. Often little folks forsook their own beds to creep into bed with other family members, comforted by the feel of other warm bodies.

During the night the frost crept up the windowpanes, painting ethereal pictures of clouds, trees, and flowers. In the morning, children drew finger pictures in the ice on the windows. As the sunlight streamed through the window pictures, it bedazzled the blanket of snow outside.

Evenings were friendly family times as they relaxed in the warmth of a cheerful fire. Cassie cut out paper dolls from heavy white paper for Julia and Victor to play with. Together they drew faces and made dresses and hats.

Lizzie retrieved corncobs from the fireplace bucket. Wrapped in a variety of handkerchiefs, they became imaginary characters in playlets for the younger ones. Julia already had a rag doll named Prudie. Sometimes she forsook Prudie for the corncob characters.

Susie the cat dozed by the fireplace. At her leisure, she came and went through the kitchen door, secure with her human family while enjoying her feline freedom.

Mother Mary and the older girls quietly pursued their needlework or bandage making for the wounded. They worked by the light of a kerosene lamp whose yellow flame burned steadily.

Father, Melvin, and Joseph were engaged in their routine gun cleaning. Dirty from powder smoke, the gun needed a complete cleaning. Melvin and Joseph sat by the hearth with the gun, a pan, a small cloth, and a greased cloth. Melvin removed the ramrod from the gun barrel and fastened a small cloth on its end. He then placed the butt end in a pan. While Joseph held it steady, Melvin carefully poured water from a teakettle into the barrel of the gun. Each took a turn rubbing the ramrod up and down in the gun barrel. With each motion, hot black water squirted out the top. With a clean cloth Joseph washed the hole where the cap was placed. With the gun still hot Melvin greased the ramrod and finally rubbed the greased rag over the whole gun. Proudly the boys returned the gun to its place above the kitchen door.

As Melvin returned to the sitting room, he moved over to the reed organ.

"It's getting late. Maybe everyone's ready for a singing time," he commented.

The family responded to his suggestion with a panorama of smiles. This was always a cherished family activity. Beginning with the lively strains of "Dixie," the music soon brought everyone to their feet to unite in song around the organ. They sang in harmony with enthusiasm:

"I wish I was in the land of cotton,
Old times there are not forgotten,
Look away! Look away! Look away!
Dixie land.

"In Dixie land where I was born in,
Early on one frosty morning,
Look away! Look away! Look away! Dixie land!

"Then I wish I was in Dixie, Hooray! Hooray!
In Dixie land I'll take my stand,
To live and die in Dixie.
Away, Away, Away down south in Dixie,
Away, Away, Away down south in Dixie."

They continued singing with strains of "Aura Lea" followed by "Yankee Doodle." Then in a more solemn tone, Melvin began playing the new Civil War song, "The Vacant Chair."

"We shall meet, but we shall miss him,
There will be one vacant chair;
We shall linger to caress him
While we breathe our evening prayers.
When a year ago we gathered,
Joy was in his mild blue eyes,
But a golden cord is severed,
And our hopes in ruin lie.

"At our fireside sad and lonely
Often will the bosom swell
At remembrance of the story
How our noble Willie fell;
How he strove to bear our banner
Through the thickest of the fight,
And uphold our country's honor,
In the strength of manhood's might."

Memories of dying sons on the battlefield flooded their minds. More than one of the family group found big tears coursing down their cheeks. Father sensed the emotions and the sad thoughts. At the end he said, "We will carry these memories for years to come and they will be a reminder of all the pain we've witnessed. Suffering brings growth. So, may we all grow into better soldiers of the Lord. Let us all kneel for our evening prayers."

From November to April, Lizzie, Cassie, and Joseph trudged a mile through the deep snow to their one-room school. Melvin had completed all the offerings in the little school—reading, writing, sums, and whatever else of knowledge the teacher was able to scavenge in the community. At home he continued his education through studiously studying the Bible and the hymnbook. *Pilgrim's Progress* and *Robinson Crusoe* were additional sources of knowledge. Never did he get enough of it.

While the work was sometimes boring or demanding for the children at school, it was great to be together with school friends. Their teacher was strict and expected high standards in all areas of work—fluent reading, accurate spelling, and correct answers in their sums. Beautiful handwriting was taught and exemplary copywork required. Cassie enjoyed spelling bees and other competitive opportunities. For others, these were occasions for pain and tears. Character traits were emphasized in their readers, so that moral instruction was built into their school life.

Cassie's eyes often wandered away from her books to rest on a quiet handsome boy in her class. If he faltered in the spelling bee, she frequently gave him hints in subtle ways. Her heart did flip-flops as she noted his beautiful blue eyes and long lashes. Even a faint smile from him sent chills up her spine. Sometimes she followed the path of his eyes and was convinced that he had been watching her. Dear heart, if only she knew that he cared! Then a sharp rap on the desk from the teacher's ruler, and Cassie's daydream dissolved into book learning once more.

On stormy winter days or too-deep snow days, the children might play at home and make snow angels or build forts for snowball battles. Sometimes the older siblings could not resist the chance for battle and would join them in the lusty snowball fights.

Without warning, it seemed that spring had slipped in overnight. Spring plowing had begun. Sensing a need for a larger corn crop, Father sent Melvin out to plow up a new field for planting corn. Cassie sought out the lamb pen again—a familiar place to meet Mandy after school.

"Oh, those pushy little lambs," said Mandy, "they just shove their wet noses right into us. It's enough to knock us over."

"Yeah," replied Cassie, "but they can't wait to suck on our fingers. I guess they never get enough sucking."

As the mama sheep hovered near her lamb, Cassie

reached over to feel her soft wool.

"Don't you just love to bury your fingers in the mama sheep's wool? It's really thick and spongy now. In a few weeks the men will be shearing them and then they'll look naked as jaybirds."

With that, both girls broke into gales of laughter. A soft rumble of thunder rolled in from the west, followed by big drops of rain that thumped loudly on the tin roof.

"Guess we better hightail it to the house!" shouted Mandy, and off they both dashed to the front porch. Dripping wet, they rushed into the kitchen, where they were greeted by the wonderful aromas of baking bread and scalloped cabbage.

That evening as the large family sat quietly around the table after finishing off another satisfying meal, Father pushed back his chair with a sigh.

"Children, maybe you've noticed that recently your mother seems more tired than usual. Yes, the days are long and there's much to be done from now on through the summer. I'm asking now for each of you to pitch in a little more. Your mother needs the help only you can give. She's in the family way and will need lots of rest. Sometimes she's sick and miserable. Remember her with the kindness she needs. It's a trying time!"

The children nodded, the older ones as if they already knew and the younger ones with a mixture of puzzlement, smiles, and uncertainty on their little faces.

The next day Cassie sauntered pensively out into the meadow, having finished her morning chores. The golden dandelions in the fields were nearly gone, replaced by soft gray feathery heads. Cassie plucked one to blow. She eyed each tiny seed as it was wafted away on the gentle breeze. Her thoughts seemed to fly with them as she seated herself on a smooth rock. The cows paused in their grass eating. Looking up, they watched Cassie, their big brown eyes sad in their lackluster faces. Clouds floated gently in the blue sky above. Watching clouds was a favorite pastime of Cassie's.

I wonder how Mama's going to get through all these months. She had such a hard time with the twins. It's like it was yesterday, so clear in my mind—all the pain and the sadness. We were afraid that Mama might leave us—so weak and tired she was. Father talked about "the valley of the shadow of death." So many mothers do not live through childbirth. Thank You, God, that Mama did get well again, but when little Wilmer died she almost gave up living too. Please, God, take care of our dear mama! We need her so much. Whatever would we do without her? I'll do my best—I'll work much harder so Mama can rest more. I'll get Mandy to do more, too.

With that, she turned to the house and the work to be done.

Chapter 3

OCTOBER 1863

"The summer work has gone well," said Father. "Each of you has pulled as a team—no slackers in this family! Our corn crop is more than enough and with our large crop of hay, the animals will be well fed. If Sam or other neighbors' crops are short, we'll be able to share with them. The Lord has been good to us!"

He said this as they assembled themselves around the long table for supper. He noted Mother Mary's discomfort as she took her place. Large with child, she moved clumsily. Her smiles were hard to come by. It was reassuring to her when she felt her unborn infant moving about and prodding her with occasional hard kicks. She smiled as her eyes met the tenderness in her husband's blue eyes. His caring support made all the difference as she bore her heaviness. Cassie gave her a concerned look, as did the others. They all knew her time was fast approaching.

To change the thinking direction and to lighten their spirits, Father again was reminded of a story:

"When I was walking down the lane
    Out of the dead the living came.
    Six there were and seven there'll be
    Give me the answer or set me free."

This one was tougher than the others—even Melvin was silent. Father waited, gazing from one to another

27

around the table, until with a smile he said:

"I heard this at the store yesterday, so you'll probably be hearing it again. The answer goes like this: A slave was walking down a lane and he came to the carcass of a dead horse. A bird had built a nest in a protected area of the carcass. After a few weeks, six baby birds were hatched. Naturally, the mother bird flew off to find worms for her babies. When she returned to the nest, she would make the seventh. Do you think the slave was set free?"

Some nodded yes, others nodded no. Father said, "I guess that's the second answer we don't know."

As the weeks wore on, Mothr Mary sometimes paced and sometimes rested. Shoes had been replaced by heavy socks, since her swollen feet and ankles left no choice— no longer could she squeeze her feet into shoes. It wasn't very cold yet, so the cold floor was no hindrance. The girls patiently went about their chores while Ella and Susan took charge.

One day in early November Mother Mary let out a little cry. It was a stab of pain—later, another.

"I think my time has come," said Mama, as her breath came in short gasps. "The pains are coming closer very quickly. After all my babies, my body is ready to deliver in a hurry. It can't be too soon for me! Cassie, run down and get Mama Sally—she'll be a big help. She's attended many childbirths and she'll know what to do. We won't call Father just yet."

Cassie ran on flying feet down to the cabin area of the farm. Rapping sharply on the door, she opened it gently.

"Mama Sally, we need you real bad! Can you come right away? It's Mama—she's having those awful pains.

She moans and almost doubles up and her face gets all twisted. I'm so scared for her. She says it won't be long now," cried Cassie.

"Don't worry, honey chile; I'll be on my way right now, so's we can get everything together. You and Mandy be on hand, 'case we need ya'," answered Mama Sally softly.

Together they hurried up to the house. Ella had put water on the stove to boil, knowing it to be a requirement at childbirth. Susan had gathered all the old newspapers that she could find. The three women hurried up to the parents' bedroom. Cassie and Mandy walked on either side of Mother Mary, giving her support as they climbed the stairs. Lizzie had gone out to find Father around the barn.

Ella and Susan arranged layers of newspapers on the bed to create a thick pad. With the girls assisting, Mother Mary settled herself on the newspaper padding. Pearls of sweat stretched in a line across her forehead as she faced the onset of each contraction. Ella and Susan took turns applying wet cloths to her face, hoping to soothe her discomfort. Mama Sally kept close watch as the birth proceeded. All watched the ordeal with anxious faces. Cassie agonized as she saw her mother weaken. Mandy had no heart for watching, so she withdrew to a corner of the room.

"It's comin', it's comin'!" called Mama Sally. "Ella, is the basin ready? Susan, have the blanket ready—this room is plenty cold."

Suddenly Mama Sally was holding the newborn up as she cut the umbilical cord. The infant let out a lusty cry.

"Glory be! You have a healthy boy," said Mama Sally as she turned her merry eyes toward Mother Mary. "He's a feisty one—tryin' to slide right outa' m' hands!"

Mother Mary lay back with a slight smile, her face resembling smooth porcelain. Cassie ran quickly to bring her a drink of fresh water. She lay so still that Ella felt her pulse. It was a very slow thump-thump.

"Miz Sally, what can we do?" cried Ella.

"Susan, go quickly, and pour boiling water from the teakettle over that purple trillium that I set out. Your mama knew she might be needing it, so it is right handy. She's a great one with those herbs, and now it may keep her livin'."

In seconds, it seemed, Susan was giving her mother teaspoonfuls of strong tea. They watched and waited with grave concern. Gradually, a little color came into Mother Mary's face. Ella checked and found her pulse thumping faster. A sigh of relief sounded around the room. Mother Mary gazed about her with a smile of gladness. Father was by her side holding her hand in his two large warm hands.

"You can't know," said Mother Mary, "how beautiful they all were—the angels that surrounded me and lifted me up, like I was leaving. Their faces were full of love and their shining garments flowed about them in delicate rainbow shades. It was heavenly!" Her face shone with exquisite joy.

"Now, you girls know your mama needs lotsa rest—you see she stays in bed 10 whole days, and then she'll need more time ta start movin' again. Jus' nursin' this baby's 'bout all she can do for a while," announced Mama Sally as she bustled about.

"Ella an' Susan, you get rid of them ol' newspapers in her bed and get some clean beddin' for her. She'll feel lots better lyin' on some sweet-smellin' sheets. Fannie, I need you ta help me get this little chile washed clean. He jus' keep flingin' his arms an' kickin', so's he's about ta slip outta m' hands. We

30

need ta wrap him tight ta keep him snuggly warm. He screamin' for all he's worth, like he plenty hungry. Mebbe he is, but he'll jus' have ta wait. Your mama's not able ta suckle him jus' yet. After she has more o' that purple trillium tea, she be feelin' much stronger. Lizzie, you keep an eye on her, give her a fresh pillow, and keep slippin' her spoonfuls o' that tea. We don' want her slippin' backward."

Suddenly Mama Sally straightened as her eyes darted from one girl to the next.

"What your mama goin' ta name this little 'un?"

The girls paused in their kindly labors as they gazed at one another in puzzlement.

"I guess we'd better call Father back," remarked Cassie thoughtfully. Off she hurried to find him.

He hadn't gone far; he was sitting in the kitchen reading the newspaper, reluctant to return to the barn until he was certain Mother Mary was out of danger.

"Father, Mama Sally wants to know what you're going to name our baby brother," Cassie said eagerly.

With an easy smile Mr. Long replied, "I guess I'd better go back upstairs and make that announcement."

As they returned to the birth room, Father reached for Mother Mary's hand. She gave him a pleased though weak smile.

"Your mother and I did talk about this in the past weeks, and we know how important his name is. It helps to make the man. We about ran out of family names, so we decided to call him Walter, a good strong name. He will be Walter S. Long."

Smiles of relief circulated around the room as this important issue was decided.

Chapter 4

While there were many hospitals for the wounded set up after the Battle of Antietam, the little Dunkard church was a possible first. In the center of battle, the little church was the closest building for serving the wounded. Benches, doors, and shutters were all utilized as makeshift operating tables. Bloodstains can still be found on benches. Cannonballs mutilated the brick walls of the church. Little remained of the once-simple sacred place of worship.

In 1851 Daniel Miller had presented to the church a leather-bound Bible. In size, it was 11" x 9" x 2½" thick. As the pulpit Bible, it was in constant use until after the Battle of Antietam. Elder Long read a psalm from it on the Sunday before the battle.

Later as a group of these faithful Brethren surveyed the damage to the church and what would need to be replaced, they discovered that the Bible was missing. They were deeply saddened. It was a symbol of all they believed in. Where could it be?

Many years passed before the story was complete.

Soldiers have always collected trophies of war or some memorabilia of a particular scene of battle. They were no different in the Civil War. Soldiers still collected souvenirs. A memento of the Battle of Antietam as a symbol of victory was a treasure to return home with.

Sergeant Nathan Dykeman, of Regiment 107, Company H, of the New York State Volunteers, claimed the Bible for his own on September 28, 1862. He and his buddy carried it home to Schuyler County in southern New York state. The Bible stayed in his family until his death in 1903. The sergeant had willed the Bible to his widowed and needy sister. Her wish was to return it to the little Dunkard church at Antietam.

In 1903 Sergeant Dykeman's regiment held a reunion at Elmira, New York. The widow told them about the Bible and her wishes for it. The men were sympathetic. They collected $10 to purchase the Bible from her and thus help her as well. Nobody knew the next step in returning the Bible.

In January 1835 John Lewis of slave lineage was born in Carroll County, Maryland. His neighbors were kindly Brethren who included him in their church family in his growing-up years. He became a member of the Pipe Creek German Baptist Church at 18 years of age.

Rumblings of war were apparent, and John headed north. In 1860 he left the area with his family and relocated in the vicinity of Elmira, New York. There he eked out a meager living for his family on a small farm. Truck gardening and marketing the produce in Elmira supplemented his income.

One day as he was returning home from market, a runaway horse galloped toward him pulling a carriage swaying from side to side. Three screaming and frantic women were seated in the carriage. Mr. Lewis quickly halted his wagon by the roadside, leaped to the ground, ran forward, and grabbed the horse's bridle. Courageous and strong, he succeeded in stopping the runaway horse, and thus safeguarded the three passengers from serious injury or death. Imagine their gratitude and relief!

The three women were wealthy Mrs. Charles Langdon, her daughter Julia, and a nurse. They lived nearby on the Quarry farm. General Langdon was not at home, but when he returned, he graciously presented Mr. Lewis with a check for $1,000. The Langdons were the parents of the wife of Mark Twain (Samuel Clemens), who was visiting at the time. In gratitude Mr. Clemens presented Mr. Lewis with $50 and a set of his signed books. The women had been visiting in the nearby Crane home, so Mr. Crane presented John with a check for $400. Not unmindful was Mrs. Langdon. She presented John with a massive gold watch with the following engraved on the inside:

"John T. Lewis, who saved three lives at the deadly peril of his own, August 23, 1877. This is in grateful remembrance from Mrs. Charles Langdon."

Mr. Lewis paid off his farm debt and became the employed coachman for the Langdon family for many years. He became a close friend of Mark Twain's.

Members of the regiment in New York heard that John Lewis had come from Maryland and was a member of the German Baptist Church. He was contacted. He had kept in touch with the Brethren through church periodicals. He told them that the Dunkard church still existed. The regiment entrusted John with the task of returning the Bible to the church. It had been gone for more than 41 years.

The Bible was again placed in the church, where it stayed until 1914. Souvenir hunters were still active, even removing bricks from the walls of the little church. Services were held only monthly in the church, and Brethren feared losing the Bible again.

They placed it in a vault at the Fahrney-Keedy Home near Boonsboro. Later Mr. and Mrs. Newton Long became custodians of the Bible, since Mrs. Long was the great-great-granddaughter of Daniel Miller, the original presenter of the Bible. (It is now on permanent display in the museum of the visitors' center at the Antietam Battlefield.)

A short distance from the David Long farm was the College of St. James. It had received its charter from the Maryland State Legislature in 1844. Members of St. John's Episcopal Church in Hagerstown had purchased 20 acres of ground, including the mansion formerly owned by General Samuel Ringgold. Quite wealthy, General Ringgold had purchased 17,000 acres in the area in 1792 and named it Conococheaque Manor. The manor house was named Fountain Rock for the wonder-

St. James School, an elite Episcopal preparatory school, the oldest boys' boarding school in the country.

ful spring nearby. It still supplies all the water for St. James School today.

A legend of an Indian princess is still alive at St. James School. She had been kidnapped from her tribe. In trying to escape from her captors, she fell exhausted at the edge of a rocky ledge. Nearly dying from thirst, she looked down and saw the rocks below her separate and sparkling clear water burst forth as a fountain. When she returned to her tribe, she led them to the spring, which they named *bai yuka* or fountain rock.

The school was founded as a church-oriented school with high academic standards. Part of the mansion was re-designed into a chapel. It was known as a Christian home for the children of the church during their education. Each new student was required to bring testimonials of his "orderly and virtuous character."

Grammar school students were required to learn in Latin six books of Virgil's *Aeneid,* Sallust's *Cataline,* and *Jugurthine War* as well as the Gospel of Matthew in Greek, and algebra. In their college years, students studied Hebrew, French, German, two classical languages, astronomy, book-keeping, ecclesiastical law, anatomy, and chemistry.

Each student was required to make 22 recitations in class every week. Each lesson lasted two hours, one hour for preparation and the second for recitation. Once a week students were called to assembly. There, each boy's studies and behavior were publicly rated from a scale of nine downward. Disorder marks were given for absence, tardiness, and disorder in class.

As an Episcopal church school, St. James had requirements for Sundays as well—attend morning prayer at 9:00

a.m., then prepare lessons in religion, attend litany and prayer at 11:00 a.m., recite sacred lessons in the afternoon, and finally attend evening prayer.

School ran from October to August. Tuition was $225. A boy's wardrobe included eight shirts, six pairs of stockings, six handkerchiefs, six towels, night clothing, and outer clothing. Note: no underwear.

The first headmaster, John B. Kerfoot, instituted a two-year college preparatory course to accommodate the many early students from the Deep South who were poorly prepared for college work.

On September 16, 1862, Kerfoot, then president of St. James School, along with Falk and Henry Edwards, rector of St. John's Episcopal Church in Hagerstown, went to Boonsboro carrying bandages, spirits, biscuits, and tobacco to care for the wounded at South Mountain. When they heard the booming of the cannon on September 17, they went to the Smoketown Hospital carrying supplies.

On September 21, 1862, Kerfoot conducted services for President Lincoln when he visited the camps near Sharpsburg. On September 24 Kerfoot visited the head-quarters of Major General Fitz-John Porter at the Stephen Grove home, where he read the service and preached the sermon. The general's mother was matron at St. James School, and a grandson was on the faculty. From there, Kerfoot went to McClellan's headquarters and read evening prayers.

In July 1863 the school stood in the direct line of fire between the Union and Confederate forces. In 1864 Kerfoot and Joseph Coit were arrested and held as hostages by the Confederates, then paroled a few days later.

Only a small number of students remained, since most of the students enlisted in the Confederate Army. The school closed until 1869, when it was reopened with Henry Onderdonk as headmaster.

Chapter 5

1864-1865

With solemn faces Cassie and Mandy relaxed on the porch steps after evening chores were finished, and began talking about how life had changed since the big battle.

"That Emancipation Proclamation from President Lincoln is got to be a good thing," announced Mandy, "but lotsa folks don't pay it no mind. People say they's still sellin' slaves down there at Sharpsburg on that ol' slave auction block where we was sold, and only 60 miles from Washington, D.C.! 'Course we are so lucky. We be free, but lots of 'em are still bound to their masters. It's like some people never heard of the freedom law. Funny thing, that house on the same corner was a hidin' place for runaway slaves headin' for Canada. A stop on the Underground Railroad is what they say.

"If'n there's anybody I'd like ta know, it's that Harriet Tubman. She's got to be the bravest woman ever lived. She's not afraid of anybody. I hear she went south 19 times and freed 300 slaves. My mama tol' me Miz Tubman was the most outstanding conductor on that Underground Railroad. She escaped to freedom when she was 'bout 25 years, but risked her life many times after that to help other slaves, including all her family, to be free. She knew all the connections and struggled through the woods and mud at night in all kinds a' weather—winter and summer. Her

39

clothing got torn in shreds, she sometimes had no food, and if she did, she shared it with the poor slave she was helpin'. Sometimes she had ta cross streams and even rivers, always managing ta fool those angry men that was tryin' ta track her down. She got lotsa beatin's and got hit in the head with a heavy lead weight when she was tryin' ta help a slave. Nothin' stopped her from bein' the 'Black Moses' of her people.

"That's like Moses in the Bible, who led his people outa the wilderness. Southern plantation owners knew 'bout her and offered a $40,000 reward for her capture. During the war she served as a nurse and worked as a scout for the Union Army. Now she's tryin' ta make a home for

Old Slave Block. Located on the southeast corner of Church and Main streets in Sharpsburg, Maryland, this block of stone symbolizes the entire Civil War. First used in 1800, it was operated until 1865, despite the bloody conflict that gripped the nation during its final years and the fact that it was north of—yet only 60 miles from—Abraham Lincoln's capital. It is believed to have been the northernmost slave block in use at that time. The auction block long shared its corner with a two-story frame house that was a hiding place for runaway slaves en route to Canada—a house that was built about the same time that the slave block was set up.

some of those poor ol' folks that were slaves and don' have a place to go."

"I didn't know you could make such a long speech, Mandy," answered Cassie. You're really letting your feelings out. I guess I didn't know you thought that much about the slaves, since you're free. But then, why wouldn't you? You know your own pain and the suffering of your parents before you came here. I can still see those welts on your father's back from all those beatings at the auction.

"Since Maryland is a border state, that puts us right in the middle of all the hate. Slaves hear stories of freedom in the North, and the smartest ones want a chance at that freedom for themselves. Some slaves have even killed their masters to be free. Some owners have been wiser and willing to help their slaves to freedom. There's something called manumission, which meant the owner would set a slave free at a certain age. Some could earn money and buy their freedom or some masters would free slaves in their final will. Of course, other slaves have been running away since they're so close to the border. It will take a long time for everything to work out. Slavery has lasted 250 years. The trouble now is that many freedmen are homeless and have no jobs. Many suffer from starvation and disease.

"Still, things are starting to get better. The newspaper said that the Department of the South decided to give abandoned land to ex-slaves. Each family will get two acres where they can plant corn and potatoes. The government will supply tools, and the family will raise cotton for government use. Still, there's not enough land because the government sold some when people didn't pay their taxes."

"That's good," Mandy replied," but lotsa families

have been separated as slaves and first they have ta find each other. Some never will. They'll just keep huntin' and huntin', not knowin' if they're even still alive."

"You're right, Mandy," answered Cassie. "It's really sad, but many people do care and are doing what they can. There are some places in the South where a superintendent of Negro affairs has been appointed. In the North, commissions have been formed for Negro relief. There are schools in Washington for refugees. Northerners are enthused about education of Negroes. A thousand young Northerners have gone south to teach ex-slaves and take care of them. There's a Freedman's Bureau, too, that is working hard on education. The Negro churches are helping, too."

"Guess what!" announced Mandy. "I hear there's a school for Blacks starting at Williamsport. Ain't that somethin'? Maybe I'll go ta school after all. I'm old ta start, but I bet I could catch up real fast."

"Sure you could, Mandy. That would be so great! We could share books, and once you start reading, you won't want to stop. You're really smart, and you'd love learning all about numbers and writing and countries and spelling and other things, too."

"I don't know. It's a long way ta walk—in winter and all—maybe five miles. I dunno. I guess it matters some who else is going," mused Mandy.

"Now, wouldn't that be perfect if some nice boy were walking your way and you could walk to school together?" replied Cassie, giggling.

"I'm pretty choosy," Mandy said, smiling. "Tisn't just any boy I'd be walkin' with every day. He's gotta be very special."

Smiling dreamily, Mandy continued, "He needs to be tall as I am, wearing a big smile that lights up his whole face, chocolate brown skin, eyes that dance when he talks and that look right at me like I'm the apple of his eye. He has to be smart, so's we can talk sense to each other. He gotta be strong, with hard muscles—I don't want no weakling. He'll have ta work hard to make a livin' for our family."

"Whoa, Mandy, you're jumping way ahead. You're talking like you're going to marry this boy, and you're not even 14 years old yet!"

"That's OK, Cassie. It don't hurt none to dream, does it? And anyhow, if'n he's the right one, I'll want to hang on ta him before some other girl turns his head. 'N' the best way to do that is to get some preacher ta tie the knot. Fifteen isn't too young to marry. I can do most anything now that a wife has ta do. 'Course that's awful young for a boy—he's not even grown up yet. Oh, well, you can't say I'm not a-lookin' ahead."

From the kitchen came Mother Mary's gentle voice, "It's time to ring the dinner bell, girls."

With that, Cassie and Mandy dashed off to grab the rope attached to the large black dinner bell. Each one yanked hard as they pulled together. The bell clanged loudly and urgently, with only brief intervals between the earsplitting clangs. When the men hurried from the barn, the girls dropped the rope and broke into gales of laughter. They had created an imaginary emergency with the rapid bell ringing and tricked the men once again.

Later, as the family was gathered around the supper table and prayers had been offered, Cassie turned to her father.

"Father, Mandy and I were having a long talk about how

it is with slaves now since President Lincoln's Emancipation Proclamation. She says slaves are still being sold."

"Yes," answered Father. "I hear that's true, but it's also true that many have been given their freedom. For some, there're more problems than before. Most of the 4 million Negroes are still in the South without land, money, or jobs. The South has been totally devastated by the Union Army—lands have been wasted, public and private properties burned, and families, White and Black, scattered. Great suffering continues in the South, and there is no civil authority to create some order. The Richmond *Times* says suffering in the South is greater than anytime during the war. Corruption is rampant and political chaos exists everywhere. Some in our government think seceded states should be punished.

"The North is surviving well. Steel factories are in big production, railroads are expanding, and cities, both new and old, are bustling. The North is demonstrating the triumph of industrialism over the agrarian way of life."

"It seems we're right in the middle," added Melvin. "I hear the governor has offered a $50 reward for the arrest of the two people who burned two churches that were being used as schools for colored children.

"Jacob Miller reports that there are still Union soldiers passing through the Sharpsburg area—sometimes in large companies. When I was at the store in Downsville, I heard quite a story. Two women, Mrs. Rench and Mrs. Darnel, came from Shepherdstown in a spring wagon. They were on their way to Boonsboro to buy goods. The Renches' little son was driving the horse. They passed some Unionists. Three of them went roundabout and waylaid them. Two pounced on them with their revolvers and swore if they made a noise they'd put a ball through them. They took hold of the horse and led him out through a field where they couldn't be seen. They ordered the three travelers to get out of the wagon and go their way. Then they plundered the wagon, took it down the creek, and left it in John Benner's field below William Otto's place. They put the horse in John Sniveley's field to pasture and for safekeeping. Later the horse's owner heard where he was and went and got him. When the robbers heard the horse was gone, they called on Mr. Sniveley and demanded pay for the horse. It seems there's a lot of such robbers around town.

"Over in Williamsport there was a great row on Saloon Row. Fifteen or 20 people were involved. Stones were thrown, five shooters were drawn, there were a number of fistfights, and of course, a lot of oaths, threats, and blasphemies were heard.

"There's a report that the Copperhead newspaper in Hagerstown has failed. I guess they meant well in trying to help the Negroes in the South, but probably didn't have enough support."

"Yes," said Mr. Long. "There's not much law and order even in our own state, but hopefully this war will soon be over and some of these problems can be dealt with. Our honorable governor Bradford did a great thing when he issued his proclamation of December 7, 1865, as a day of general thanksgiving and prayer. While most people will be loafing, hunting, or butchering, it's still a step in the right direction. Regardless of what is happening around us, and there are plenty of stories to be told, we must keep our faith and move forward. We can't right all the wrongs, but we can be a light in the darkness."

Chapter 6

"Mandy, have you noticed how Fannie just goes mooning around like she never has her mind on anything she's doing?" inquired Cassie as they sat peeling potatoes for supper.

"I sure have," answered Mandy with an emphatic nod. "She's like in a daze—sometimes I don't think she even knows what she's doin'. I bet she's still thinkin' 'bout that Union soldier, Frank. You know what we heard him tell her."

"Do I!" replied Cassie. "I couldn't believe he'd be so forward. He was here only two days, and it was like he already made a marriage proposal. Of course, Fannie just ate that up. I think she's been goo-goo-eyed ever since!"

"Well, if you ask me, I wouldn't trust a Union soldier, 'specially one that's been way out in Kansas. Why did he leave home in the first place? Mebbe he had a fallin' out with his fam'ly. And a soldier! He prob'ly killed a lot of people. Then he came back home when he didn't have any money—doesn't sound like a great husband choice to me," commented Mandy.

"It must be being in love, as they call it," responded Cassie. "You'd think she'd have forgotten him by now. Maybe he said the same thing to other girls he met. Why hasn't he sent her any letters? If he really cared about her, he'd have gotten a letter through to her by now."

"He's gotta be a lot older than she is. I wonder if she knows how much," remarked Mandy. "I can't see why she'd want anyone who's losin' his hair a'ready. She be really silly—should be lookin' after some 'a the nice boys in church and forget the likes 'a him."

"I guess it doesn't much matter what we think; she's not going to change on account of us. I guess it was what they call love at first sight. Remember how she just fixed her eyes on him and they were all glazed over and how she laughed louder than anyone else at his stories," concluded Cassie with a toss of her head. "You'll never see me carryin' on like that!"

Fannie wandered into the kitchen, her face unsmiling and her eyes averted. She turned to the two girls.

"Cassie, did you and Mandy finally get those potatoes peeled? You'd better get them cooking or they won't be done in time for supper. You two do dawdle around a lot and were likely chattering on and on as usual. Sometimes I think it takes the two of you to make one of the rest of us."

"Oh, don't be so crabby, Fannie," answered Cassie. "We do just fine. It's you who seems to be out of sorts lately. What's bothering you?"

"Never mind!" retorted Fannie angrily. "You two wouldn't ever understand. You're much too young. You can't know what it's like being 16 years old."

The girls glanced at each other sidewise with ill-concealed snickers, then turned to traipse out the door.

While others in the household still slept, Fannie greeted the day in a tremble. She spotted the last fading stars and said softly, "Please, dear God, I miss him so much! I need him! Just a letter to know he's still alive. My heart aches for the sight of him, and my arms are aflame for his touch!"

Fannie paced back and forth, unable to be still as her whole body seemed to be in a state of churning. She wrung her hands together as tears streamed down her cheeks. Her anxiety had climaxed. She could bear it no longer—this dreadful uncertainty!

Somehow, as the household awakened, her feelings were forced into hiding. No way must they know how much she cared. It was her own private secret, but how to get through another day! She could not last much longer. Dare she hope? Could there be a letter today?

As the family went about their morning chores, Fannie dashed from one task to another, trying to drown her thoughts in busyness. Pans clattered as they fell from her hands to the floor, a chair fell over, and Susie, the cat, screamed a loud meow as her tail was trampled on.

Mother Mary gave her daughter an anxious look, but said nothing.

During a lull in the morning work, Fannie slipped out the door and headed for the woods. Maybe there she could find peace as the soft breezes wafted across her face and the leaf cover crunched under her feet. A gray squirrel glided through the branches of an oak tree never faltering as it did little leaps from one branch to another. A baby rabbit fixed its gaze on this intruder as it sat motionless nearby.

Gradually Fannie's inside rumblings were quieted. Nature's normalcy worked its magic to bring a gentle peace to her soul.

Resolutely she returned to the house and continued her chores.

Suddenly the kitchen door burst open. Joseph rushed into the kitchen waving his arm excitedly as he held up a letter in his hand.

"Fannie, look what I found in the mail! It has your name on it, and it came from Pennsylvania. Who do you think it's from?"

In one swift move Fannie grabbed the letter from his hand and, without uttering a word, dashed up the stairs to her room. Her hands shaking violently, she could barely manage to open the precious missive. Alternately, tears stung her eyes and smiles creased her face as she raced through the long-awaited letter. Assured of his life and his love, she began once again, this time reading more slowly.

"Dearest Fannie,

"I hope you haven't forgotten me. I certainly haven't forgotten you! You've been in my dreams so many times that I can't count them. I wish I could have written much sooner. From your home we moved on to Gettysburg; there I wasn't as lucky as I was at Antietam. I got a buckshot in my arm that really laid me low. I was lying on the field for hours before anyone found me. By then I had lost lots of blood and was so weak I couldn't walk. Some people came with a makeshift stretcher and carried me to the nearest hospital. There some kind women cleaned out my wound, removed the embedded bullet, and poured in some whiskey. A good strong drink before they started helped to deaden the pain. I guess they had some herbs like your mother has, because they mixed some up and put a poultice on my arm. I lay there for a week trying to get my strength back. I drank lots of water and ate plenty of chicken soup.

The women worked hard to take care of us soldiers.

"Then it took another week before I felt strong enough to travel. I hired a horse and wagon to make my way back to Woodbury. It was a long, lonely drive. Had you been at my side, it would have been too short. It took several weeks over rutty roads, fallen trees, and washouts from storms, but no real danger areas. I stopped overnight at farmhouses, and people were good to a wounded soldier. They fed me well and gave me a good bed.

"I arrived home safely, but still didn't have much use of my arm. It was all pretty numb and my fingers couldn't grip a pen. I've been massaging and exercising them until they're almost back to normal. My arm is still quite painful, but it's healing.

"I hope to come down to see you soon. I'll plan to drive a horse and wagon to Hancock, where I can get a train to Williamsport.

"All my love,
"Frank"

Fannie lay on her bed reading and rereading, scarcely able to contain her happiness. Yet tears flowed at times as she considered his suffering. Now, more than ever, her only desire was to be with him and share his pain.

Suddenly she slid from her bed and searched for pen and paper. How she wished for some fine linen writing paper! There was none; some lined tablet paper would have to do. His letter needed a prompt reply.

She sat down at a little table and began her reply.

"Dearest Frank,

"I think of you all the time! How I wish I had been there to nurse you back to health! I've been longing to hear from you ever since you left. With your being in the Army, I could only hope and pray for the best. Lately my faith was wavering. I began to think that maybe something terrible had happened to you. I didn't want to give up hope.

"Your letter came just in time. I was so thrilled to see your name that my hands shook uncontrollably as I tried to open it. Of course, everyone in the family wanted to know what you had to say, but I just ran up to my room and slammed the door. I had to be alone and savor each precious word. I cried when I heard how hurt and weak you were. Oh, that I could have been there!

"You can't imagine my happiness when you said you will come to see me soon. I will live to see that day.

"My family is well and will be glad to see you. We'll meet you at the station—just tell me when!

"Your dear one,
"Fannie"

Several weeks later a second letter arrived for Fannie. This time, instead of rushing to her room, she tore it open immediately, sure it would have important news. It did.

"Dear Fannie,

"I loved your sweet letter. You are definitely the sweetheart of my dreams. I plan to take a horse and wagon to Hancock on Thursday, the fifteenth, and stay there overnight. I'll need to arrange where I can put up my horse and where I can spend the night. The next day

51

I will board the train for Williamsport. I'll look for you at the station on Friday, the sixteenth.

"Yours only,
"Frank"

Fannie's face was wreathed in smiles as she jumped up and down for joy. In less than two weeks he would be here with her and her family. So much to do, so little time, and then he would be hers to enjoy!

Fannie looked about her through new eyes. Everything must be perfect for her love. Was the parlor a bit shabby? The carpet was worn and the curtains were dingy. The wallpaper was faded and loosening in places.

"Oh, Mother, how can we fix things to look better? I know we don't have much money, but our home is looking downright dingy!" exclaimed Fannie.

Mother Mary looked lovingly at her young daughter. "Remember, dear, it's not the house that Frank will be seeing. It's you he's coming to see. Most likely he'll have eyes only for you. You are right about the looks of our home. With the war and all, many improvements have had to be let go, in the house and on the farm.

"I know you'll be feeling better if you can brighten things up a bit. I do have some pretty calico that could be sewn into chair covers that would make quite a difference. If you'd like, you can tackle that project. Then, too, the curtains could stand a good washing. I'm sure you can handle that."

"Oh, thank you, Mother," answered Fannie. I'll get those curtains washed and hung out today. Tomorrow I'll heat up the irons and press them nicely. The chair covers will have to wait until next week, but I think I can get them finished in time."

That evening, as the family encircled the table for supper, the conversation quickly turned to Fannie and her last letter.

"So your soldier friend will soon be on his way," said Father, not unkindly. That's quite a wagon trip from Woodbury to Hancock. He must be a lot stronger now."

Fannie blushed prettily, choosing to ignore her father's reference to "soldier." She knew that would be a touchy issue. She hoped it would go away without a fuss.

"Father, I've been thinking," Fannie began. "Do you think maybe we could take a day off for a family excursion? They say there's packet boats on the canal now that run excursion trips. Some are overnight, but they have day trips, too. It would be so great if we could do that when Frank comes."

"Well," answered her father, "you really are full of ideas. You know we've never done that, and I don't know as we should. We need our time for work and worship. That seems rather frivolous to me. Don't you think so, Mother?" he asked as he turned his eyes to Mother Mary.

"It really is a new idea, but maybe it wouldn't hurt. We could all use some time off from all our hard work," she answered, as her eyes sparkled with the possibility.

Father didn't miss that sparkle. It was a rare look of animation that she seldom showed. He smiled warmly at the wife he so loved. For her sake, he would consider.

Chapter 7

After the Maryland campaign of the Civil War, the Chesapeake and Ohio Canal presented a scene of desolation for a distance of 12 miles. The canal was a line of supplies for the army of the Potomac and for residents of Washington, D.C. The canal also supplied coal from Cumberland for Washington. The Confederates had also destroyed much of the Baltimore and Ohio Railroad, including the B&O railroad bridge near Frederick.

More than 500 boats ran on the canal night and day, never stopping. Boats were 90 to 95 feet long with oak bottoms and pinewood sides. They were 14½ feet wide, which was a few inches less than the width of the locks. Boats had names such as *Lonely Star, Alice May, Owl Dooley,* or *Farmer's Friend.*

The boats might be filled with wheat, corn, potatoes, oats, rye, live hogs, cattle, chickens, cider vinegar, molasses, flour, cornmeal, smoked hams, crates of eggs, and wood. Boating never stopped, and weather didn't change the routine even when there were bad storms.

The barges were drawn by mules, one walking behind the other. Men were fond of their mules, keeping them clean and fat. They were good, gentle, and more intelligent and tougher than horses. Drivers would say "Come up!" rather than hit the mules. Stables for animals were maintained on the rear of barges. Two mules rested in the stables while the other two worked.

Storage for hay and surplus supplies and a cot for the hired hand were located in the hay house in the exact center of the boat. Part of the boat was a stable. Between the stable and the hay house, and between the hay house and the cabin, were the hatches that covered cargo in the hold.

There were warehouses along the way to get food for mules. Sometimes owners would speculate on hay or grain and sell some to other boat owners.

There's a story that two mules slipped overboard; several boatmen jumped into the canal and led the mules back up the bank.

Another story is about a pet goose named Jimmy, who lived on the boat for 27 years. People stayed clear of Jimmy, since he had a reputation for biting people who came too close.

Three men were needed on a coal boat: a driver, a steerer, and one to tend the team. Mule drivers walked 25 to 30 miles a day every day of the week. The pay was poor: $20 to $30 per month or $10 a month for a 15-year-old boy.

Young mule drivers often climbed on a mule's back and fell asleep. Also, they often went barefoot, since shoes wore out too fast. They often foraged food from fields along the way and shot rabbits and groundhogs from the boat.

It was a very rough life: 16- to 20-hour days seven days a week with very little sleep. The captain's word was law. Boatmen drank a lot at taverns along the route and during their stop at Georgetown.

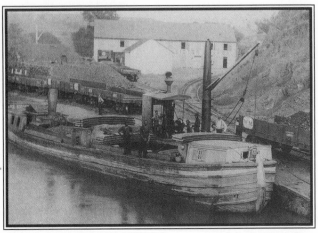

Canal boat at anchor. The main jobs on a canal boat were steering, driving and caring for mules, and cooking. Most captains and crew members could take turns at all three.

A boat traveled at the rate of two miles an hour down-stream with 120 tons of coal and three miles per hour up-stream with a lighter load. It was 185 miles from Cumberland to Washington. Usually boatmen allowed 90 hours to go down and 60 hours to return or six days round-trip. The cost of a new boat might be $1,200 to $1,500.

The captain used a tin horn to call the lock man at a quarter to a half mile away. At night the lock tender would wave a lantern to let them know he heard them. The hardest job was to steer through a lock. There were 75 locks and seven dams in all for the length of the canal. There was just six inches allowance on each side of the boat. Stone locks could tear up a boat, so the steerer had to know exactly how to enter the lock and how to stop. There was a scrubbing post with a rope around it to act as a brake when the boat entered the lock.

The captain and his family lived in the front of the barge. Housekeeping was much like living in a house. Curtains, bedspreads, and the cooking galley were similar. There was little schooling for the children. Small children were chained or harnessed to the deck for safety. The ropes were long but not long enough to fall overboard. Beds were bunks, with girls' bunks being enclosed. Boys sometimes bunked in the feed room.

Bread, molasses, and ham were staple foods. In addition, they might have cornbread, corncakes, coffee, eggs, bacon, or fresh fish, such as catfish or bass. At times, the captain swore at the cook for breaking all the dishes, and the cook swore at the captain for not buying any.

A delicacy on the captain's table was turtle soup. There were four or more species of turtle along the canal. They floated on the water or sunned themselves on the bank. By using a four- or five-foot hickory stick, a person could use the pointed socket on one end to probe mud holes. If it hit a turtle's back, it gave a dull thud and rebounded like rubber. A steel hook on the other end would pull the turtle in. A snapper can cling to a stick and be pulled for many feet. Once a captain struck a 35-pound turtle and needed help to carry it back. The snapper was slippery, always twisting its head and snapping its jaws.

Social life was limited but often involved crews from other boats. When in port, there might be all-night square dances, hoop-skirted girls, and lots of corn "likker."

Romances developed between crew members and lock-keepers' daughters. Marriage sometimes followed.

Winters along the canal were a bit unusual owing to the idleness of the boatmen. With a possible 750 boats on the canal, more than 3,000 men would be unemployed. Captains and their families often had a winter home onshore. Boathands, dockhands, lockkeepers, and warehousemen were mostly idle. Some crew members stayed on the boat all winter with the approval of the captain. Since many of these men had saved no money, they began foraging at once. Lawmen were kept busy with their petty crimes. Chicken stealing was a major violation. Crap and poker games often ended up in a brawl and a jail sentence.

An awning over the back of the boat gave the steersman some protection from rain or sun, but the mules and driver were out there on the towpath, come wind or weather.

At least 20 boats moored at Williamsport, Sharpsburg, and Shantytown. Williamsport was a desirable location because of the proximity of Cushwa and Steffey coal yards, where they could find coal for their cabin stoves. These boats were also ideal places to run off batches of "bootleg booze." "Mule kick" is what they called it, and there was ready sale for it. They could rotate their still from boat to boat, hide their mash kegs of swill in the bushes, and seldom get caught by revenuers.

The captain's families all knew about and feared Haunted House Bend. Some believed the mules felt the same way. They seemed to plod by the area hurriedly. All boatmen tried to pass the bend before nightfall.

A new captain had not heard of the "ghosts." One dark night he tied up at the "Haunted House." As soon as he turned out the lights, things started happening. The mules seemed restless. When the captain lit his lantern, he discovered that the mules were untied and floating away. He quickly called other crew members, who recovered the animals and tied them up again. The captain retired. He heard someone raising the hatches. He grabbed his shotgun, but found the hatches in place as usual. Later in the night he checked his mules and found they had eaten no grain and were prancing restlessly. Somewhat later a young mule driver told the captain that he had tied up at "ghostly bend" and he'd better get away fast. They moved quickly. A mile ahead all was quiet, and they could finally settle down for a few hours' sleep.

The accepted story was that fierce battles were fought there during the Civil War. Many on both sides were killed. The dead were buried without markers. The belief was that ghosts of the dead caused the restlessness among the living, if anyone dared to stay overnight.

Packet boats were trim pleasure craft pulled by three or four horses. They were painted white on the outside with red or green window trim. Larger than commercial vessels, they carried passengers only. They were tended by trim, young uniformed men.

Railroad passengers traveled by boat to Point of Rocks and then transferred to rail for Washington, D.C. They operated on time tables from town to town. A small room in front served the crew. Another small room served the women. The main cabin included the dining room and parlor, which also served as the men's sleeping area. The kitchen and pantry were in the stern.

People slept on narrow cots of canvas with straw pads for mattresses. The cots were supported by iron rods attached to the sides of the boat and ropes hanging from the ceiling. Some people slept on the floor.

People sat on the deck during the day. As they floated leisurely down the canal, they were entertained by wildlife on the shore. Black bears, mountain goats, bald eagles, groundhogs, raccoons, and possums, as well as all kinds of birds, were to be seen cavorting along the way. Less appealing were the water snakes and black snakes. Wildflowers, including arbutus and flax, added to the scenic interest. While a boat was passing through a lock, people could leave the boat, go for a brisk walk on the towpath, and catch up at the next lock. People didn't need to feel hurried; they could get off to fish, hunt, sketch, or maybe study plants. It was a leisurely ride.

Chapter 8

An excursion on a packet boat—it seems like a worldly thing to do, thought Mr. Long as he pondered this possibility. There's much work here that needs to be done. How can we leave it for a whole day of pleasure? If it were helping a neighbor in need, there would be no question. That's our Christian duty—to help one another. But then, my dear Mary looked so eager and she works from dawn to dusk every day of the week. Even on Sunday she pauses only for the time of worship.

We men do get a break from our routine during the winter months—no hard fieldwork, just simpler jobs like making repairs, greasing harnesses, checking traps, or shelling walnuts. Then I go off on a number of preaching missions, meeting new people and seeing lands beyond our home. She stays home with all the cares of homemaking and family.

Yes, it would do her a world of good! She would delight in the change of pace; the freedom from home cares. Seeing new faces, hearing the variety of bird calls, and reveling in the exuberance of wildlife along the canal would give her gentle spirits a lift for sure.

Mr. Long entered the house with a kindly smile and a peaceful heart, knowing he had made a right decision. He surprised Mother Mary as his long strides brought him to her side. She turned from stirring the stew over the hot stove to meet his smile. In an unusual gesture of affection, he embraced her warmly and added a quick kiss on her soft cheek.

Cassie watched in amazement. What's come over Father?

she thought. *Something special must be happening. I wonder if it's about an excursion.* She hurried over to Fannie's side, where she was peeling potatoes.

Speaking almost in a whisper, Cassie asked excitedly, "Fannie, do you think Father may have decided to go on the excursion? He seems especially happy about something."

"Oh, I do hope so," whispered Fannie, her face radiant. "It would be the perfect way to spend the day with Frank! Cassie, will you be nice and finish peeling these potatoes? It's time for Melvin and me to start for Williamsport. We've got to be there before the train comes into the station. I want to be right on the platform as he steps down from the train."

"Yes, it's no big thing, and I know you're riding on a cloud, but you're heading for big trouble. You know how Father feels about soldiers and war. You'd better not get your hopes up too high!"

Fannie left quickly without a word, dashing upstairs to change into her Sunday dress and add a few curls to her hair. She must look her best to meet Frank. Her heart beat rapidly as the time drew near for their meeting.

After a quick change, Fannie rushed outside and rang the dinner bell to call Melvin from his chores. Early that morning she had impressed him with the urgency of their trip. Melvin hitched the horses to the light two-seated wagon that would carry them to the train station in Williamsport. Climbing up beside Melvin on the wagon, Fannie uttered a "let's go," and off the horses trotted. It was a beautiful autumn day and the horses knew the way with Melvin doing little more than holding the reins.

Fannie sat quietly, absorbed in her own hopes and

dreams, scarcely aware of the bright birdsongs, the soft wind in the trees, or the dust rolling up behind the wagon. While it was little more than a half hour's drive, it seemed to Fannie like a lifetime.

"Can't we go faster, Melvin? I'm afraid we won't get there before the train. That would be awful if I wasn't there to greet him," she pleaded.

"You sure are keyed up about this Frank. You met him only the one time, and he's been in another big battle since then. He's years older! What makes you so sure that he's the right one for you? After seeing all those soldiers killed and killing some himself, how can he be a good husband?" asked Melvin.

"Oh, you'd never understand, Melvin," Fannie retorted. "All you care about is work and books and music. I wonder if you ever look at the girls. Plenty of them look at you with hopeful smiles, but you turn away from them as if you don't care."

Melvin blushed but made no response. It was something that troubled him, too.

Soon they were pulling up to the station platform. Fannie, holding up her long skirt, leaped lightly from the wagon. No train in sight yet. She waited impatiently as she paced back and forth.

Melvin found a hitching post for the horses and wagon. Leaving them, he ambled into the station for a chat with the stationmaster. He certainly didn't want to be in view when Frank stepped off the train.

Finally a train whistle sounded, still at some distance. Fannie's heart beat so fast, it threatened to burst out of her bosom. She paced the platform even faster, oblivious of the half dozen other people waiting for the train's arrival. Louder and still louder the whistle sounded as the engineer began braking the train. Slower, yet still more slowly, came the engine until it rolled to a grinding stop.

As the conductor stepped down from the train, Fannie's feet fairly flew to the open door. Her eyes were pinned to the doorway. One, two passengers alighted— three, oh, it had to be Frank. He was changed! He looked older, a few gray hairs and such sadness in his face.

As he stepped down, he saw her—his Fannie. They fell into each other's arms. Tears of joy mingled as they held each other close.

Gently pushing her away, Frank gazed long and hard at the girl he could only dream about until now. No, she hadn't changed. She was beautiful, tender, loving, and everything he remembered.

Fannie's eyes warmed with compassion because now she knew how much he had suffered. Hair can gray overnight when great pain is present. Now his sadness turned to joy as he feasted on her gentle smile and her eyes, which spoke only of love.

Hand in hand they walked toward the station, meeting Melvin as he emerged from the doorway. A formal handshake between the two young men, and they were off to the horse-drawn wagon.

Melvin loosed the horses and climbed into the driver's seat. Fannie and Frank had already arranged themselves on the second seat, not close enough to draw unwelcome stares as they drove through town.

As they rode through the countryside with hands entwined, Fannie and Frank spoke in low tones of first his train ride and then his long wagon ride from Woodbury to Hancock.

"It was rather uneventful," Frank said. "The weather was pleasant, and the roads were in fair shape. It was a long walk for the horses, but I rested them at times and found water for them to drink. They'll be in good shape for our return trip."

"I'm so glad you got here without any mishap. I understand there's still an Indian tribe along the way. I hear they're usually friendly, but a lone traveler could make a good target," cautioned Fannie.

"Oh, I steered clear of them; I wouldn't want to take chances, especially in good hunting grounds in the mountains. It's best not to disturb them," responded Frank.

Upon reaching the Long farmhome, Fannie and Frank proceeded to the front door, while Melvin unhitched the team. Mother Mary waited at the open door to welcome their visitor. Frank returned her gracious greeting and felt a warm acceptance.

Soon they were all seated around the well-laden dinner table. Fannie noted that her mother had brought out their best tablecloth and company china. She beamed a happy smile at her mother. *She really understands,* she thought to herself.

The conversation soon drifted to the Battle of Gettysburg. The family knew little of events there, since their local newspapers covered mostly local news or news from Washington, D.C.

Mr. Long's face fell as he heard of more devastation and many more lives lost. Frank sensed a growing tension and uneasiness as he continued his stories. Finally Elder Long could listen no longer.

With trembling voice and furrowed brow, he asked, "But why must this bloodshed continue? What do we gain by killing our brothers? Our church does not believe in war. We believe in settling our differences by peaceful means. If any one of our members takes up arms, they are no longer a member of our church."

Frank looked around the table—all eyes were turned his way, awaiting his reply.

Fannie could only stare at her plate with down-cast eyes.

"I didn't know, sir, that you felt so strongly on this matter," replied Frank. "No, I do not like the killing and am sorry for any suffering that I caused. It seemed to me a just cause. Slaves need to be free. They are human be-ings—not to be bought or sold. When I returned from Kansas, it seemed my civil duty to report to the Union Army. I did my best, beginning as a private and moving up to the rank of major. We all suffered hunger, exhaustion, and intense pain for a cause we believed in. Many gave their lives, but I guess I was one of the lucky ones."

There was a space of silence.

Cassie spoke up.

"People have different beliefs. Frank did not grow up in the teachings of our church. I don't think we should condemn him."

Mother Mary smiled wanly at Cassie. She too had grown up in a different faith, but she knew it was her duty to be submissive to her husband and not to question his beliefs. Fannie gave Cassie a grateful smile as the tension eased around the table.

"True," said Father, "it is not for us to condemn, but we

serve God through the church, and we will abide by the rules of the church. I believe Frank needs time to think this over. Fannie, let not your affections control your conscience!"

This last was too much. Fannie burst into tears as she shoved back her chair and fled from the room.

The meal was completed in silence, each one searching for his or her own truth.

Later, as chores were completed, the family again assembled in the parlor for their evening family worship. It was a sacred time at the close of each day. It was a time of praising and thanking God for the blessings of the day. Requests for a peaceful night of rest and His care for the coming day were also included.

Frank joined in the family sing as Fannie slipped in beside him. Melvin lightened the solemn mood with a few lively numbers on the organ. After the final prayer was said, Father raised his head, gave a thoughtful glance around the room at each of his large family and finally at Mother Mary.

With a smile he said, "You all are very dear to me, but most of all your mother. She has given you life and constant devotion day after day and year after year. No sacrifice is too great and no task too hard—all without a word of complaint.

"For her sake, I've decided that a day off is in order. Tomorrow morning we will hitch up the wagons and head for Williamsport. I think the packet boat will board the passengers about 9:30 and be ready to leave by 10:00.

"Girls, you will need to prepare a lunch for the family to take with us on the boat. The weather is promising, so it should be a good day for travel."

With this announcement, children and grown-ups alike could barely contain their excitement. A spontaneous clapping ensued.

After getting past her own shocked delight, Mother Mary went into action. An hour until bedtime, and preparations needed to be made. Dresses pressed, shoes shined, and baths to be taken. *Thank goodness today was baking day,* she thought. *We'll have fresh bread and fry up some ham. Those cookies that Ella and Susan made will be a tasty treat while we munch on some apples. We'll need a large container of water for an all-day trip.*

"Melvin, bring a ham from the attic and see how quickly you can saw up enough slices for frying. Ella and Susan, you're in charge of frying the ham; you may have to build up the fire, and we'll need a few loaves of bread sliced up. A small crock of apple butter can go along for the little ones to have apple-butter bread. I think we'd like a jar of pickles, too.

"Fannie and Lizzie, you check the dresses, but first put the irons on to heat, because some will need pressing.

"Cassie, you get the little ones started on their baths, so they can be soon to bed.

"Joseph, you're the shoeshine expert, so get started on your job and Melvin can help when he's finished slicing the ham. Everybody! Bring your shoes to Joseph for polishing. We must look our best for such a special day!"

Mother Mary sank back in her chair, exhausted with the suddenness of it all. Still, she smiled and her eyes danced as she turned to her husband.

"Oh, David, I can't tell you how happy I am. It will mean so much to all of us to go floating down the canal and not have any work to do. It will be a day long remembered. I can hardly wait!"

Mr. Long returned her warm smile, confident he had done a good thing.

As the morning dawned, its light filled the home with happiness. From the youngest to the oldest, they bounded from their beds with bubbling enthusiasm. Dressing was accomplished in record time. Chores were dispensed with quickly as a burst of energy seemed to infect each one. No dillydallying today! The little ones were beside themselves as they sensed something unusual. Mother Mary's voice took on a rare sharpness as she tried to quiet them to eat a hearty breakfast.

Nine o'clock arrived, and they were in the wagons and on their way. The frenzy of excitement had now subsided as the horses trotted briskly down the country road. Cassie chose to ride with Fannie and Frank in the second wagon while minding the little ones. That didn't stop her from keeping one ear tuned to any snitches of talk between Fannie and Frank. Her curiosity about their love life was keener than she might care to reveal.

Soon they arrived at the boat dock and hurriedly piled out of the wagons. About 25 other people were lined up to go on board, some of the women in fancy colorful dresses and hats, with their men in morning coats and top hats. It was a gala affair. The Long family by contrast appeared modestly dressed even in their Sunday best.

Exploration of the boat was the first order of the day. The children dashed madly hither and yon followed by many warnings of not going too close to the edge. Mother Mary held tightly to little Walter's hand.

Melvin was not long in locating the organ, and soon the air was alive with the strains of "Maryland, My Maryland." "Yankee Doodle" followed, with young people falling into a marching pattern around the deck.

The shore abounded with a veritable chorus of sounds—shrieking jays, mockingbirds, barking dogs, breaking of tree limbs, baying of foxes, or melodic bird-songs. Wildflowers along the banks were a rainbow of color interspersed with majestic green ferns. Tall trees became a canopy over the seething life of the forest.

How peaceful! How perfectly lovely! thought Mother Mary as she sat complacently in her canvas chair, hands folded in an idleness that she rarely enjoyed. Mr. Long's attention was centered on the horses and drivers as well as the makings of the boat. Fannie and Frank sought their own private retreat area, preferring their own aloneness. Cassie rode in the rear, preferring to watch the waves as they kissed one another.

It was a totally satisfying day and one that would stay in the memory of each one for many years.

Chapter 9

It was a crisp autumn day when Frank prepared to return to Woodbury. He hitched the horses to the wagon, since Melvin was already in the field plowing. He must get an early start in order to reach Woodbury by nightfall.

Fannie did not smile; thoughts of his leaving were too painful. Each day of his presence was a glowing thing—like mellow gold it seemed. His leaving would darken her days. How could she bear it? Their days together were convincing. They were meant for each other. Of course there would be letters—maybe every week. She would live for those and read them over and over again. Somehow she would have to survive until his coming again.

Father had been adamant! They must give their love time to grow and mature. Haste was not wise. How could he know how much they loved each other? Maybe he was the one who needed time to be convinced.

Fannie walked slowly toward the wagon as her thoughts tumbled crazily about in her head. Cassie followed her more rapidly. She would go for company instead of Melvin. She was more than glad to offer to go. This "love" thing began to fascinate her. She could really see how much Frank and Fannie meant to each other. To her, it still seemed strange, but she was ready and eager to learn more about it. No longer would she take it lightly.

They climbed onto the wagon seats, Cassie on the second seat as the quiet observer and Frank and Fannie in front with hands linked tightly. Few words were spoken as the horses trotted jauntily through the countryside, heads held high. Cottony clouds floated through an azure sky and there was the lowing of cows in the pasture and birds swooping overhead, yet the travelers were oblivious of these things, so deep were their thoughts.

As they pulled into the station, they could see the engine chugging down the tracks, its shrill whistle blowing. Frank tethered the horses, then reaching for his valise, he prepared to board. Fannie was quickly by his side, holding his hand. At the final moment they fell into each other's arms, unconcerned with the onlookers. Cassie had not left her seat on the wagon; she couldn't miss this parting. As Frank climbed the steps, Cassie took off for a quick walk before the return trip. Fannie gazed long and hard as the train picked up speed, waving until it was out of sight.

The sisters walked slowly toward the wagon. Cassie untied the horses, but Fannie quickly took the reins. Tears streamed down her cheeks as she guided the horses homeward. Cassie sat wordless, wondering how she could comfort her sister. It was a new almost grown-up feeling. Now she knew she would be kinder to Fannie, more aware of her sister's heartache.

When Fannie and Cassie arrived home, they were bombarded by work to be done. Each member of the family was needed in the project of the day. Today it was apple butter and cider making. Better to finish up all the apples today than delay until they were not usable. Like autumn leaves ripped from their branches by high winds, the girls' thoughts of love and romance were blown from their minds. Practical matters of preserving food for the winter claimed their unwilling attention.

The menfolk had just arrived from the orchard with bushels of the last apples of the season. Many had been lying on the ground with either brown spots or worm holes. No matter—it was quantity rather than quality that was of consequence. A few worms would simply add food value. Nobody ever reported illness or stomach problems from eating a wormy apple.

The apples were unloaded from the wagon near the springhouse. Tubs were filled with water to wash the apples. Some of the leaves and dirt were loosened in the water and skimmed off after the washed apples were removed. Washing apples was a fine job for the younger children. Stooping was easy, washing was easy, and occasional water play encouraged them to continue.

Mr. Long and Melvin manned the homemade cider press. Apples were fed into the hopper and ground up. The "mush" was then fed into round cages containing slotted, wooden flats covered with burlap. A circular metal plate on top pressed down the flats until the apple juice was squeezed through. Since the press was hand-powered, it was an arduous and time-consuming task to make a year's supply of cider.

The cider was stored in the cellar or put in the flowing spring water. Fresh cider was a tasty drink in ample supply for all the family to drink their fill. As cider aged, it acquired a tang and eventually became hard with an alcoholic content. A nip of hard cider was not unusual for the menfolk even in a religious home. Much of the cider was stored in a barrel to turn into vinegar. Vinegar had many uses in a nineteenth-century farmhome. As a regular table condiment to flavor vegetables or meats, it was also thought to have health and healing qualities. It was useful as a household cleaner, was not hazardous, and would keep forever.

Nearby, the women were "snitting" apples with flying fingers. For apple butter, they removed stems and seedpods, peeled and quartered them. Several bushels of apples must be prepared for an all-day cooking. A large copper-lined iron kettle hung over the open fire. The women filled the kettle with apples and cider. Sugar and perhaps spices were added. Copper-lined kettles helped to prevent apples from sticking and burning. Still, regular stirring with a wooden stirrer was necessary. Even Julia was big enough to take a turn at stirring the apple butter. As the fire burned low, wood needed to be added throughout the day.

The wonderful aroma of apple butter cooking and cider making was a fitting reward on a crisp fall day. What fun it was to view crocks of fresh apple butter stored in the cellar for lusty appetites on the frigid days of January. Fresh bread smothered with apple butter was unsurpassed for an afternoon snack.

With the chill of winter coming on and the inevitable drafty rooms, wet feet, and childish forgetfulness of the need for outer wraps, soon illnesses became the order of the day. When cold weather hit, grippe was not far behind. First one then another complained of being hot and then shaking with uncontrollable chills. Mother Mary laid her soft hand on a warm forehead and was quickly aware when a child was feverish. Little ones persisted in keeping on moving until they wobbled unsteadily on their small legs, then toppled to the floor tearfully.

AFTER ANTIETAM

Mother Mary had developed her nursing skills and knew that bed rest was a necessity. Many cold damp cloths did she apply to feverish brows. A comforting hand was medicine itself, but the wet cloth helped to lower the body temperature. Weakness, aches, and pains were characteristic of this illness. No doctor was called, because they had no cures. Mother Mary offered her medicinal herbal teas, which often brought relief. The illness was very contagious, so often several family members lay miserably sick at one time. Mother Mary was ever faithful in attending to their constant needs, ignoring her own aches and weariness. Adults were not exempt from the illness and sometimes, too weak to stay on their feet, were compelled to seek rest on a straw mattress for several hours. Chores were held to a minimum and often approached with dragging feet. Pneumonia was a fearful and often fatal illness that often followed the grippe. Care was taken to not get chilled further and to get plenty of rest.

Sometimes with young children the illness was followed by whooping cough, a frightening disease and also contagious. Spasms of coughing followed by deep horrific sounds when drawing air into the lungs were scary to both the victim and others in their presence.

Reports of a scarlet fever epidemic in the community also intensified the anxiety in the Long home. It too was extremely contagious, and already several children in the family of Alfred Sharman had died of the dread disease. It was best to avoid contact with other people, since no one knew exactly how the disease spread from one household to another.

Cassie had no heart for watching all the misery of the

little ones in their illness. It was too dreadful—their hurting, their crying, their gaunt little faces after refusing to eat. Mostly she left the household behind to spend time at the barn with her beloved animals and the daily chores. Guiltily she told herself that older sisters were more able to help than she was. She didn't dare imagine what it was like for her poor mother.

Why, she thought to herself, *does all this illness have to be? It doesn't do any good, and it makes so many people suffer. It seems that God doesn't care. If He did, He would wipe it all out. He seems so far away!*

It seemed that winter would never end. The food supply had dwindled until Mother Mary could not stretch it much longer. Watered-down soups, stews, or potpies were merely tolerated, but stomachs needed to be filled.

Then came the awakening. As the sun slid over the horizon a little earlier each day, spirits lifted. The cold, cruel winter eased into the brightness of spring. Frost-hardened ground softened, readying itself for plowing and planting. Early spring flowers poked through the sod giving promise of new life and nature's abundance. Delicate bluets and pink meadow rue blanketed the pasture. Tender dandelions were lavish for the gathering—a delicacy after the scarcities of winter. Mother Mary delighted in arousing jaded appetites in the springtime. She was sure to please with a great bowl of dandelions smothered in a bacon/vinegar dressing, garnished with slices of hard-boiled egg.

By the month of May the earth was warmed, the frost had passed, and spring planting was at its busiest. Cassie reveled in the planting of flowers. She carefully turned over the soil by the porch, then placed the plants in small holes and patted the soil firmly around each one. Some six weeks before, Mother Mary had prepared for this time by going out in the chill weather and sowing seeds in the cold frame—a box-shaped device topped by old windows where seeds would be encouraged by the hot sun on the glass warming the soil and holding the heat during cool nights. In this way vegetable plants as well as flowers would get an early start. Cabbage, tomatoes, sweet potatoes, and lettuce were all pushing up against the glass, eager for their new outdoor environment.

Cassie loved this time of year—the greening of the landscape, leaf buds on the trees sporting myriad shades of pinks, greens, and yellows. Birds had returned and were singing their joys of nesting and a profusion of juicy worms and delectable insects. Cassie was more than willing to forsake the kitchen chores and spend her days in the freshness of spring.

It was a time for thinking, and Cassie loved to let her mind wander while her fingers were occupied. *God made such a beautiful world—His creation is mind-boggling, from the heavens above to the earth beneath and everything living between. Who is He? Where is He? I guess He's in the air I breathe. Why did He place me here? What plan does He have for my life? I am only one, and I wish I knew exactly where He wants my life to go. Now, there's Fannie—she thinks she knows. That seems nice, and she seems so happy with Frank, even when she reads his letters. Is there someone special somewhere for me? I feel some strange longing. I don't understand it. It's like a gnawing-away at the strings of my heart. If only I knew. Maybe that's where I must be patient. It's not going to happen the way it has with Fannie. Sure, there're some nice boys at church, but no one seems special. They're friends I've always known. I guess I could marry one of them. They seem to like me. I wonder when and whether I'll be sure like Fannie seems to be.*

I have more lonely times now, as though I need someone to share my thoughts. Mandy and I are not so close now that she's going to school. She's getting lots of ideas and is really boy crazy. I suspect she'll find her one and only and be getting married soon.

Her thoughts continued as she finished her planting, climbed the porch steps, and let the screen door slam.

She stared long and hard at the girl she saw facing her in the mirror above the washbasin. *Am I pretty? My eyes look dull, but I can brighten them when I smile. My nose is definitely too big, but what can I do? I'll work on my smile. It's not bad, and if I laugh, my eyes start dancing. Good! I'll try that. I think boys like that. But my hair—oh, I must leave the braids behind. I'm much too old for braids. They make me look like a little girl.*

She dashed upstairs for some pins and returned to her mirror reverie. Arranging her two braids to encircle her head, she pinned them tight and smiled her approval. Now she was sure to be noticed. In minutes she had left her girlhood behind and transformed herself into a young woman. She stood straight and tall with her head held high.

Chapter 10

1865–1872

Late in March, Susan was the first to leave the security of home and family to start a home of her own. Eli Yourtee was a farmer and a member of the Brownsville German Baptist Church, later to be chosen as an elder in that church. He was 10 years older than Susan, but that was of no great concern to Susan or her family. He was of good character and, in Susan's opinion, quite handsome. Being older meant simply a greater maturity than other choices she had considered.

She assumed they would settle down on a farm near her parents or maybe his family, as the custom was. That was not to be. Eli had grown restless. Crops were still being confiscated by troops lingering in or passing through the area. Both families had suffered heavy financial losses. Besides, he had heard of the wonderful farmland in Kansas. Other families had already gone west, weary of the devastation of their homes and farms. Letters with good reports of the opportunities in Kansas were discussed occasionally at the country store.

As Eli reasoned, now was his chance to start a new life, an adventure into the unknown. Susan was not enthusiastic. It was a frightening possibility. She knew that travel that far was hard and dangerous; Indians still roamed much of the area. Some were hostile. How could she leave her beloved family? Without her mother to guide, whom could she turn to, especially when she learned she was pregnant. There would be months of travel and settling down.

Eli listened to her fears, but assured her of his constant support in this leap of faith.

Others had gone, arrived safely, and found success. So would they! They would leave at the first signs of spring. Susan knew that a wife did not question the decisions of one's husband. She offered no further resistance. With a heart overflowing with sadness, she prepared for the parting. When the day for leaving came, Susan surveyed her home with tearful eyes. What memories! Her childhood frolics, their close family working together from season to season to provide food, the sings around the organ, the church meetings in their home, and the agonies of a bloody battle—the good and the bad. All of it, she must leave behind.

As the family had all assembled, she moved slowly around the circle, hugging each one hard, not wanting to let go. Mother Mary held her close, with tears streaming.

Eli called to her that the horses were ready. Susan turned to her husband and with a hint of a smile walked out the door and did not look back.

Cassie came running toward the house from the mailbox, waving a letter in the air. Gasping for breath, she dashed into the kitchen.

"Fannie, there's a letter for you today—probably the one you've been dying for. You must open it quickly and see what it says."

Fannie needed no prodding. Her hands shaking as she grabbed it quickly, she found scissors to cut off the ends.

Just seeing Frank's handwriting gave her heart palpitations. She read the lines quickly, since his letters were usually brief and pointed. He would be arriving in Williamsport in a week from his writing.

"Oh," exclaimed Fannie, "that's three days away. I'm so excited I can't think straight. That's so much sooner than I dared hope. He can't come too soon for me, but there's much to do before he comes. Cassie, please help me with some of the extra chores. We don't have Susan now to help, and Mother is always overworked."

Cassie noted Fannie's energy burst and her flushed face. Fannie had seemed so dreamy some days and sort of lost. That letter certainly made her come alive.

"Yes, I'll be glad to help, because there's no way you can get all the baking and extra cleaning done by yourself," replied Cassie.

Bread and pies to be baked, curtains to be washed and hung, and lots of extra cleaning to be done were just some of the extra chores that needed doing. Fannie must give a good impression! She let Cassie choose her jobs, since any extra work for Frank's coming would be not a burden to Fannie but a pleasure.

On the appointed day, Melvin again drove Fannie to the station. The train pulled in, and Fannie was first at the open door. Wreathed in smiles, they fell into each other's arms. As Fannie drew back, her sparkling eyes noted a healthier, stronger Frank than before. Arm in arm they climbed into the wagon and headed for home. Everything was the same—no questions between the young lovers. Time had altered nothing. They were in love and meant for each other.

That evening around the table, greetings were exchanged between Frank and each member of the family. Visitors from afar were an event in the Long home, a break from the humdrum of their daily lives. There was an air of lively anticipation as Frank shared his experience while traveling from Bedford County, Pennsylvania. He held up his arm to demonstrate his added strength.

"My arm is almost back to normal," Frank said. "Exercise, good food, and time have made me a lot stronger. I feel as though I can conquer the world now."

Mr. Long smiled kindly.

"It's good to see you've overcome your injury. Many were not so fortunate. It seems that nothing has changed between you and Fannie. I can't doubt your love for each other. If you marry, where would you plan to live?"

"Since I was here last, I have purchased some land of my own," answered Frank. "I'm interested in fruit growing, so I've already planted a hundred trees—apple, cherry, and peaches. Frost can be a problem there, but usually it doesn't come as late in the spring as farther west. I may need to use smudge pots when there's a late frost. It's a new idea, but I think I can manage it. There aren't many growers there, so there should be ready sale.

"As for where we'll live, I'll need to find a house until I can build on my own land. I'm sure I can find a suitable place. Morrison Cove is a prosperous area with a number of churches and good people."

Mr. Long listened carefully.

"It sounds to me as though you're thinking ahead and doing good planning. Marriage is a serious lifelong commitment for better or for worse."

He turned to Fannie. "Fannie, do you think you can be happy that far from your home and family? You know how hard it was for Susan to leave. Kansas is farther away, of course, and we may not see them again. Still, Bedford County is a long way from home, and as little ones arrive, you may not get to see your family either."

"Oh, Father, I know I'll miss you all very much, but I'll have Frank every day. That's where I belong—by his side. Then too, I've already thought of the pain of leaving, so I've asked Cassie to go back with us for a visit," answered Fannie.

Mr. Long chuckled. "I see you've taken care of everything, even your own homesickness in a new place. You'll need help in getting settled, so even though we need Cassie here, you'll need her more," he said.

Fannie and Cassie exchanged excited smiles. The two of them had so much to talk about that clearing the table and cleaning up the dishes was a welcome chore.

"I can't believe Father was so great about everything. Not a word was said about Frank being a soldier, and he was so stubborn about that before. I guess he sees we're good for each other and so much in love. I think he really likes Frank and believes he'll be a good husband for me. My heart is near to bursting with happiness!" exclaimed Fannie.

"I'm glad for you—you've waited a long time. You'll have plenty to do before your special day. We'll have to plant more of everything so you'll have provisions to take with you. How many dresses are you going to need? You know you're allowed to be more fancy for your wedding— some lace and tucks and a pretty shawl. Then you will need linens for your hope chest. I know you have some already, but you'll need to do lots more needlework."

"Yes, I have been working on my tablecloths and napkins, but I still have doilies and dresser scarves to finish. Since the church made rules last year about how we can dress, I can't be as fancy as I'd like, but I have some ideas."

That evening after the others had gone to bed, Fannie and Frank stayed on in the parlor, looking into their future together. First: When and where should they marry?

"I'll need time to find a house and some furnishings," announced Frank. I want my wife to have a home to come to. Then you can add your special touches when you get there. We may be lucky enough to get a family started soon, and then you'll be more than busy."

"Oh, Frank, you're so thoughtful and good to me—I can hardly wait, but I know I must. I'm not even 19 yet, so I have so much to learn. We'll have to grow more food and prepare it to take with us. Then I have an endless amount of sewing and needlework to do. Maybe we should wait until fall."

"That sounds good to me," replied Frank. "I'll have a lot of orchard work as well, as I'll need to earn some money before we marry. Do you think you can be ready by early November?"

"That's just perfect—I'm sure Father would like us to wait some months. He still thinks I'm pretty young to leave home. Could you come down and we be married in my home? I'd like Father to marry us. He marries most of the couples around here."

"Why not? Now that he accepts me, I feel quite at home here. There's nothing I want more than to see you happy."

"Then it's all settled," said Fannie, smiling merrily.

"It's all so wonderful—I feel as if I'm dreaming, and yet I know you're right here beside me. It won't be long until we'll always be together. That will be heavenly!"

She nestled her head on Frank's shoulder, and he encircled her in his arms and held her close.

One evening about a month after Frank's visit, the family attended a special revival service at the Manor church. Brethren were there as well as a sprinkling of others from the community.

One young man seemed to stand out from the others—maybe because he was alone rather than with anyone. His dress was as a "man about town" rather than accepted Brethren garb. Pleasantly friendly, he was clean-shaven and of medium height. Ella had met few suitable young men and was well on her way to spinsterhood. While she accepted this with a submissive spirit, she had not given up hope.

When she saw John Remley, her eyes sparkled with pleasure as a smile played about on her lips. John responded to her interest directly.

In the German Baptist churches, there was always a divider in the church between men and women. This continued on the outside during their social exchange. They did not mingle.

John, being unaccustomed to this tradition, did not hesitate. He walked across the grass to where Ella was standing, tipped his hat, and reached for Ella's hand. Her face reddened, but shyly she reached to accept his firm handshake. He introduced himself, and Ella gave her name and with a sweep of her hand indicated her family connection. It must have been the right timing for both of them. John asked Ella if he might see her home, and with no further acquaintance she followed him to his one-horse carriage.

On a clear crisp evening with a rising golden moon, how could any young couple not have romantic feelings? Conversation flowed easily and time was happily forgotten. John reined in his lively horse to prolong the homeward trek. The full moon moved just ahead, guiding them on this magical journey.

It was late when they arrived at the Long homestead. The house was in darkness—too late for any further visit, since John still had far to go. He leaped from his carriage and helped Ella from her seat. Together they walked to the door, where plans were agreed on for the future.

Quietly the mutual attraction blossomed into a serious courtship. Ella kept her own secrets, not wanting affairs of her heart to become family discussions. Father and Mother Mary did not pry or require her to explain. At age 24 Ella was a grown woman.

One rainy summer evening when chores had been lighter than usual, Ella was ready to open her heart.

"Father, you've all been aware that I've been seeing John Remley now and then. We are both the same age and—and—well, I guess we're in love. We think alike and feel so good with each other. He grew up in Greencastle and attended Iron City Commercial College in Pittsburgh. He came here for a teaching job and has taught at Antietam and Williamsport. Now he's applying to Hagerstown Academy, since it pays better. Someday, he hopes to study law." She paused. "He has asked me to marry him, and I said he would need to ask you."

This was a long speech for Ella, so she looked longingly to her father for his favor.

"That was wise of you, Ella, even though you're past the age when it's expected. Parental approval helps a marriage to get off to a good start. You've always been grown-up in your ways, probably because you're the eldest and were needed to help at a young age. Now it's your turn to move out on your own and make decisions.

"John seems like a likable young man and an ambitious one. I like to see that in the young. He may go far. Bring the young man to see me and I'll give you both my blessing," Father assured her with a smile.

Ella smiled happily, filled with gratitude.

"John's ready anytime, but I need a little more time, and we'll need to find a place to live."

She looked to Mother Mary for some answers.

"Ella, it's really up to you, but I have an idea. Maybe you and Fannie would like a double wedding. The time seems about right for you both to get everything prepared. Fannie, have you and Frank set a date yet?"

"Yes, we have, Mother, and I hope it's all right with everyone. November 23—after the fall work is over and before the snows come. We'll be leaving the very next day."

Turning to Ella, Mother Mary asked if that would suit her and John. Ella nodded in quick agreement.

"It will be so nice to plan it all together and invite some friends to come, too," she added.

Fannie looked relieved, knowing her older sister could always be counted on to handle anything.

Chapter 11

During the Reconstruction period, the country moved toward a more powerful position in the world economy. By 1866 the South had accepted the responsibility of governing their people. Southern Black Unionists reported that "we are being waylaid and slaughtered as though we were wolves" and looked for presidential elections to improve their lives. Attempts were made to guarantee that all federal offices, including post-masters in the South, be Unionists and anti-Ku Klux Klan. By uniting with Unionists in each Southern community, order would slowly be restored.

Complaints against rebel officials raising taxes were justified. In one year, taxes had increased from one third to double the year before. The legislature was accused of outrageous extravagance. Offices were created for ex-rebels that were unnecessary, thus creating debts of millions of dollars. A turnaround occurred in servant jobs. Before the war, Blacks held most servant jobs; after the war, Whites had become the servants.

Farmers in Washington County had great losses. In some cases, after they submitted a list of losses, payment was made. Other farmers sued the government to recover losses. Often a major question was whether the loss was the responsibility of the rebels or the Union Army.

In the meantime, life moved on and recovery was

gradual. A severe drought one year destroyed crops and pasture. Mills were unable to run. One winter was so cold that potatoes and apples froze in the cellar, and pumpkins froze in the bedroom. Farmers continued to plant in faith that "next year will be better."

Melvin was now a young man and interested in the changes in his community. One of his regular nights out was the Debating Society held in the Odd Fellows Hall in either Boonsboro or Hagerstown. He readily took his place in the front of the hall where the participants sat behind a long table. Speeches were timed and points were given. Sometimes local issues were debated; other times they debated political issues/national issues. Not only was this a challenge to Melvin's quick mind, but a way of serving his community. Presenting both sides of an issue was thought-provoking to the audience and often cleared the air. Melvin's father was a well-respected member of the community. While Melvin was young, his views were accepted on his father's reputation. His own wide reading had gained him a wealth of knowledge that others found hard to match.

Another of Melvin's interests was the singing school, which he organized in the local school. The room was quickly filled one evening each week. Whether some came more to hear Melvin's sweet tenor voice than to learn their do-re-mi's is unknown, but it was a popular social event.

Temperance in use of alcoholic drinks was a current concern of the time. Speakers traveled from town to town. A temperance lecture was held in Williamsport with Leonidas Alen as speaker. There was a huge turnout, and many informal debates followed.

Revival meetings were also an occasion for socializing. Mr. Unro, a Lutheran preacher, held a series of meetings for four weeks. It brought in some of the worst boys in town. Town became much quieter for a time. Thirty or 40 young people were added to the church.

Since shopping was done rarely, each store stocked a variety of goods and thus became a general store. Walker, Mill, and Company was typical: sugar, syrup, molasses, tea, coffee, cheese, flour, fruits, fresh oysters, pineapples, brandy, foreign and domestic liquors, salt, phosphates, feed, twine, ropes, and halters were all available. Washington House dry goods store ordered from New York and Philadelphia wholesalers. They stocked silks, wools, ginghams, velvets, denims, mourning fabrics, tickings, pillowcases, napkins, laces, shawls, and hoopskirts for misses and children. Men's pants sold for $1 to $5 and coats for $1.50 to $8. Aughenbaugh Apothecary carried patent medicines, Indian vegetable pills, lamps, oils, paints, and stoves—coal stoves were $26 to $65, cookstoves and parlor heaters $45 to $60. Old copper, lead, and iron were bought or accepted in exchange for work.

At home, Melvin became the official bearer of news to the family. Shocking was the story of Benjamin Long, a distant cousin, who was in court almost every year. He was accused of sending his slave to burn his brother Simon's barn as well as neighbor Claggett's barn. His second wife moved with the children to Kansas while he was in jail, where he eventually hanged himself.

The railroads played an important role in the economy for transporting goods, mail, and people. Seven or eight freight trains from the west came into Ellicott Mills every 24 hours. They picked up dry goods and groceries for all points west. Many were the railroad stories. One man, Patrick Garrett, a 24-year-old brakeman on the Baltimore and Ohio Railroad, slipped when switching cars and fell from a car across the track. He was cut to pieces by the wheels passing over him and instantly killed.

Occasionally, when work was slack on the farm, Melvin headed for Williamsport and the canal boats. It was a diversion and a source of personal income at the same time.

Melvin had continued to take every opportunity that became available to educate himself. Naturally his career interests led him into education. He completed two years of study at the Maryland Normal School. This prepared him for teaching locally. A few years of this and he was ready for a new adventure. A private school had been operating in the south end of Hagerstown. It closed for lack of students and was offered for sale. With David Long's keen interest in education and his lack of opportunity for any formal schooling, he was always supportive of Melvin's interest. Together they purchased the property and reopened the school. Melvin soon became principal and named it Linden Seminary.

Later, he pursued a teaching position at Brethren Normal School (now Juniata College) in Pennsylvania. There Melvin was much admired by female students. He was referred to as "that good-looking little Long that walks with a limp." After marriage, he moved to Trappe, Maryland, where he continued his career as principal in public schools.

After Fannie's wedding, Cassie traveled with the newlyweds back to Woodbury as planned. Wanting to look her best for her first train ride, she wore her newest dress with off-the-shoulder puffed sleeves and narrow white standing collar trimmed with a black velvet ribbon at her throat. She had coiled her shiny brown braids around her head, looking every inch of her 16 years. Her eyes danced with excitement as she boarded the train.

Cassie had distanced herself from Fannie and Frank so that she could more easily observe the other passengers. The car was not full, but young and old as well as several young families were a challenge to Cassie's imagination. What were their stories? Why were they traveling and would they return? Questions continued to rummage her mind. Sitting near the back of the car, she could not see their faces. She must be courageous.

Rising from her seat, she walked slowly and sedately forward, wearing her best smile. A few heads turned and returned her smile. As she reached the end of the car, she paused, turned, and retraced her steps. With subtle glances as she moved down the aisle, she noted a few young men, but saucily lifted her chin and avoided eye contact. Their snickers followed her. Fine! She now had faces to add to her daydreaming in this all too short ride.

At Hancock the sisters climbed into the wagon while Frank hitched up the team. Cassie sat on the second seat and observed the scenes on her right and on her left. Deer darted across the dirt roadway and into the forest, foxes and rabbits crossed their path, and the trees, now bereft of their leaves, swayed gently in the wind. Soon the horses slowed as they struggled up the long mountain toward the road to the west. It was a ride to be remembered.

Several years later Fannie issued a desperate call for

help. It had been a long hard winter. Both small children had been ill with a series of illnesses; first, the too-familiar grippe, then the scariness of whooping cough followed by measles. Fannie was tired to the point of uncaring as she expected her third child. She pleaded with Cassie to come and stay at least a month before the new arrival. Cassie was reluctant, but out of loyalty to her sister she agreed to go and help.

When she arrived bubbly and energetic, she was dismayed to see her still young sister looking much older and weary beyond belief. The children were pale and thin with sad little eyes.

"Oh, Fannie," cried Cassie, "I didn't know things were this bad or I would have come sooner. I feel great, so you take it easy and life will be looking up in no time."

"Cassie, you can't know how glad I am to see you— it's such a comfort to have you here. I felt I couldn't go on much longer. The baby is due soon, and the little ones aren't very strong yet. Then Frank wants to leave after the baby is here and move to Kansas. The fruit business hasn't gone well, and he thinks we can do better there. Several late frosts have destroyed half the fruit. He just can't get ahead. He's really discouraged. I'm not much help to him when I'm down, too."

"Well, we know Mother had some really hard times— during the war and all. But it must have been her faith that kept her going. I guess we just didn't realize how hard it was for her," answered Cassie. "I'm glad I'm here for you now and before you move; I can help you get ready for your trip, too."

She reached to give Fannie a warm hug.

The next day was Sunday, and they all piled into the wagon for the two miles to the little church. It was their one social contact for the week and always eagerly anticipated. The novelty of a different community and meeting new people made Cassie's blood race a little faster. Would there be a someone? Sometimes her curiosity threatened to overtake her good sense. She must be careful—not too forward, but not too shy.

As they entered the church, Cassie's quick glance spotted a young man sitting alone. After being seated, Cassie could wait no longer. To her sister, she whispered urgently, "Who is the young man sitting alone? What's his name? I never saw him before."

Fannie turned to Cassie with an amused smile. She knew her sister's impulsive nature and how impatient she could be. She answered in the quietest whisper she could manage.

"His name is Seth Myers. He's visiting here today. His wife died about six months ago. He looks mighty lonely to me" (this with a twinkle in her eye).

Cassie could barely contain herself during the service. She kept stealing glances at this new prospect. This was not without results. Some kind of mental telepathy comes into play when one person frequently eyes another. Seth moved uneasily and then turned his eyes toward Cassie. Her eyes quickly found the floor. But soon she stole another look. Fannie nudged her, thinking she was being too obvious.

After the service Frank met the visitor at the door. He quickly introduced his family and his wife's sister who came to help them. With a smile, Seth greeted them warmly, then turned his attention to Cassie. After a few inquiries about her stay, he suggested that he see her home.

Cassie responded with, "Oh, I'd love that! I'll be at Fannie's house a long time; this will be a nice change. Thank you for asking!"

They walked slowly toward his team and carriage, finding conversation easy. On such a beautiful day, Cassie was unaware that the drive back to Fannie's house was a longer different way than their drive to church. Cassie was riding on a cloud. She believed without a doubt that she had met her "someone." Older than she, yes, but she liked older men. They didn't do stupid things, as some young men she knew did. He was thoughtful, he smiled easily, and he was fun to be with. Not bad to look at, either.

Chapter 12

Upon Cassie's return home to Maryland, she lost no time in getting a letter off to Seth. She had so much to tell him about her venturesome trip home and all the happenings on the farm. Again she was uneasy. Sometimes her eagerness got out of bounds, and if her daydreams crept into her letters too much, Seth might back off. *I can't risk that,* she thought. *I really do like him a lot, but he's so much more mature than I am. I must seem like a silly girl to him. Still, I know he's lonely and maybe I'm just what he needs.*

She sent the letter off, and before it could possibly have time to reach him she was checking the mailbox daily for the answering letter. About two weeks later her answer came. Cassie was always first to the mailbox. When she saw Seth's name and the return address, she jumped for joy while her heart did flip-flops. She ripped the envelope open with her fingers rather than waiting for a knife-edge opening in the house. With a quick glance, she noted the well-formed, even script and eagerly rushed through the first reading. With his three terms at Shirleysburg Academy, Seth was better educated than most young men in his community.

Cassie felt proud to receive such a beautiful letter. It was a first. None of the boys she knew would or could write such a letter. She continued into the house, holding the letter almost reverently as her thoughts tumbled helter-skelter in her head.

I'm still in my teens—am I really ready to think of getting married? When I see Fannie's hard life, I'm not so sure. True, she adores her dream guy and will follow him wherever he wants to go. I don't know if I'm ready for that. Here, there's always work to do, but Mother is still the one who's in charge, and that's fine with me. I still have lots to learn.

Seth must really miss his wife. He looked pained when he mentioned her, so they must have really loved each other. Can I take her place? Can I be what he wants and needs?

Absentmindedly she strode into the kitchen, where she found a quiet corner. Mother Mary looked up from stirring the potato soup on the stove.

"I see you have a letter in your hand, Cassie. Is it from who I think it is?"

"Yes," answered Cassie, "and now I must be alone for a while to read it very carefully and sort some things out for myself."

"Of course," replied Mother Mary. "It's a very wonderful thing to think about."

Cassie opened the letter again thoughtfully.

"Dear Cassie,

"You were a breath of fresh air in my life. I only realized how lonely I've been since losing Catherine. Your enthusiasm and joy of life lifted my spirit more than I can say. I really miss you and find it hard to keep my mind on my work. I really enjoyed meeting Fannie, Frank, and their children. In fact, I went over to Woodbury church on Sunday, and they invited me home for dinner. They are a fine Christian family and will be missed when they leave for Kansas.

"I'm enclosing a newspaper column that Frank wrote called "Woodbury Kid." I thought you and your family would find it interesting.

"Crops are doing well, so it's a dawn-to-dusk life on the farm, as you well know. Then I must cook my meals and do other household chores.

"When the harvest is over, I would like to take some time and come down for a visit with you and your family. Do you think they will have me? I hope you can convince them. I want to spend more time with you. I'll be waiting eagerly for your letter in reply.

"Sincerely,

"Seth"

Cassie sat dreamily, chin propped firmly on her hand as she held her precious letter. She turned toward Mother Mary.

"Seth would like to come down for a visit after harvest is over. What do you think?"

"That sounds like a fine idea to me," her mother answered. "We'd certainly like to meet this young man before anything serious might develop. Your father is a pretty good judge of people, and I know you'd want his approval."

Cassie dashed over and gave her mother a warm hug.

"I've been thinking a lot, and I really need you both to help me think through this. I'm not sure I can be all he wants in a wife. Maybe I'm not submissive enough."

Mother Mary smiled fondly at her outspoken daughter. With merry eyes, she replied, "Submissive you are not,

Cassie, but some men like women with spirit. Just don't pretend to be something you are not. You might succeed for a while, but the real you would soon be out with it. Your impulsiveness is so much 'who you are.' We love you for being Cassie, and I suspect Seth is feeling this way, too."

"Oh, Mother," answered Cassie, "you always make me feel better when I'm confused. It's so wonderful to grow up in a loving family, and that's the kind of home I want to have. Nothing is more important!"

Letters continued to travel back and forth between Seth and Cassie at almost two-week intervals. Cassie ardently anticipated each cherished missive. At the same time, his words always bothered the edges of her mind. Mostly, her questioning mind said, *Am I good enough? Am I grown up enough? He seems very serious and expresses deeper caring thoughts than most young men. He certainly isn't like the farm boys I know.*

The Williamsport, Maryland, train station. Cassie and Fannie married men from Pennsylvania. When they were courting, the men would take the train to Williamsport, where the young women met them in a horse-drawn wagon.

Finally, the long-awaited letter arrived giving a date for his visit and his arrival time. Cassie's excitement mounted daily as the event grew closer. Sometimes flustered to the point of forgetfulness or clattering dishes, Cassie was lost to her family. Each one granted her space and only met each other's knowing eyes.

When it was time to hitch up the horses for the drive to Williamsport, it was Father who readily stopped his work to take the reins. Always they were close—as close as a father and daughter might be. Mr. Long was charmed by Cassie's effervescent personality and now wanted to support her in her frenzied state.

As they rode along the dusty road, Mr. Long easily led the conversation, while Cassie was unusually quiet.

"I'm looking forward to this meeting just as you are, Cassie, though certainly not as much. You haven't told us much about your young man, so I'll almost be meeting a stranger. I know he farms and has lost his wife. Apparently he's a churchgoing young man and has an education. He's a number of years older than you are and probably feels the need of a wife as early as possible. So far, so good. Have you noticed any weaknesses?"

"Oh, no, Father. He's all the good things," replied Cassie. "He's thoughtful, hardworking, speaks and writes well, and is so much better than other young men I know. I just don't know if I can measure up."

"Stop worrying your pretty head about that right now, daughter. If he's all you say, then you're not far behind. Even if you have to stretch a bit to keep up, you're equal to that, too. Girls seem to mature faster than boys of the same age, and you've taken lots of responsibility at home since your sisters are gone. He'd be a very lucky man to gain you as his wife."

"You're just too kind, Father, but you do give me more confidence and you're almost always right about everything."

They rode on in silence until they reached the station. The train whistle sounded in the distance as they drew up to the hitching post. As the wheels of the train ground to a halt, Cassie searched for the open door. Seth stepped down from the platform, and in seconds Cassie flew into his waiting arms, nearly sweeping him off his feet. Mr. Long walked slowly forward and smiling, he extended his arm for a hearty handshake. The two men's eyes met in warmth and understanding.

Together the three walked toward the waiting horses and light wagon. Mr. Long waved the couple into the second seat as he picked up the reins. Cassie and Seth, oblivious of everyone and everything but each other, rushed to tell each other of their adventures both in travel and at home since their last letters. Every detail seemed important to share with the other.

Arriving at the homestead, Mother Mary welcomed them warmly while heavenly aromas issued from the kitchen. She ushered Seth in where the table was already spread for family dinner. As his eyes passed around the circle of smiling faces, Seth noted that all eyes were centered on him—a bit overwhelming, but pleasurable, too, in their acceptance.

Conversation soon turned toward farming comparisons between Morrison's Cove, Pennsylvania, and Washington County, Maryland.

"Brethren are always looking for good farmland, and we've heard that Morrison's Cove has some of the best farmland in Pennsylvania. Of course, we think we're not far behind here in Washington County. Limestone soil is topnotch for crop production, even though we do have to work around the rocks," offered Mr. Long.

"Yes, some of the prettiest farms I've seen are in Morrison's Cove," replied Seth. "But then, I don't live there—I'm farther east in the mountains, Aughwick Valley near Shirleysburg."

"Then how did you happen to be at Woodbury church when Cassie was there?" inquired Melvin.

Seth laughed. "Oh, that's easy," he said. "I decided that it was a good time to visit other churches and maybe meet some nice young lady. I think the good Lord led me there that Sunday."

Cassie blushed as Seth turned to her with a smile and a twinkle in his eyes.

"Then too, I'm thinking of volunteering for the ministry, so I need to learn more about the churches in the area."

There was a general silence until Mr. Long nodded his approval.

"That's a worthy calling for a young man, Seth, and with your education, hard work, and good character, you have much to give."

Everyone around the table seemed to give a nod of approval. Mr. Long's dedication to ministry and good works were well known and respected in the community as well as by his family.

That evening, Cassie and Seth remained in the parlor after family worship—glad to be alone with each other.

They watched an ember smoldering on the hearth while a few flames jutted upward, persistently proclaiming new life. Holding hands with occasional caresses, it was enough just to feel the nearness of each other.

Cassie felt a warmth and a feeling of peace such as she had never known. To her, it was a sign. She felt in her heart that she now knew God's will for her life. Seth, too, felt a rightness, a comfort that he had not felt for many months. Time seemed to stand still for both of them.

Mother's Clock

A youth sat on a sofa wide,
Within a parlor dim;
The maid who lingered by his side
Was all the world to him.

What brought that glad light to his eye—
That cadence to his tone?
Why burns the lamp of love so high,
Though midnight's hour has flown?

The clock above the glowing grate
Has stopped at half-past ten;
And, long as that young man may wait,
It will not strike again.

The artful maiden knows full well
What makes the clock act so,
And why no earthly power can tell
The time for him to go.

Cassie suggested they go outside to watch the stars for a time. As they looked deep into the night sky, the millions of stars were overwhelming in their numbers and brightness. They held each other close as they sensed the wonders of the universe. An owl hooted "who-oo, who-oo," breaking the stillness, but only adding to the beauty of the night.

Seth reached for Cassie's other hand and turning her gently to face him, with lips almost touching, he whispered, "Will you marry me?"

"Oh, yes!" was Cassie's ready response.

They lingered in a loving embrace, until the chill air finally drove them inside. Sleepily, they bade each other a reluctant "good-night."

After Seth's leaving, Cassie moved through her days with a changed outlook. She found that to love lightened her load and gave value and direction to her life. Her future was decided. Her efforts were now a preparation for that future.

They set the date for their wedding in three months. Cassie insisted that Seth bring his parents and others of his family who could manage to come to help celebrate their marriage. Most couples had a simple service at the home of the minister. Cassie wanted it simple, but felt the presence of both families would give more support to the new couple.

The wedding day dawned with the good fortune of delightful fall weather. Seth and his family had arrived the day before. The house was in readiness, and Elder Long was smiling broadly as he anticipated the nuptials for his favorite daughter. The families assembled in the parlor, all dressed in their Sunday best. Mother Mary looked pleased and comforted. It was a lovely feeling day.

When the final "I do's" were said and sealed by a kiss, tears of happiness streamed down Cassie's flushed cheeks. She felt herself dissolve in brightness as her eyes moved from one dear face to another. Then she grasped Seth's hand, and with stately poise, never before held, she walked quickly toward the doorway and her new life.

Epilogue

Catherine (Katie) Long Myers was born in 1851. She married Seth Myers from middle Pennsylvania in 1872. She was his second wife and nine years younger. They had six children, several of whom died young. Son Howard became principal of Hollidaysburg High School in Pennsylvania. Seth was called to the ministry two years after their marriage. They served churches in German Valley, Aughwick, and Altoona, Pennsylvania, and in New Jersey for six years. Catherine died in January 1903.

David Long was born on Jordan Road near Hagerstown, Maryland, on January 29, 1820. He was the son of Joseph and Nancy Rowland Long. His grandfather, Isaac Long, came from Germany. David's education was very limited, but he studied a dictionary zealously to learn about words. At age 30 he was called to the free ministry and ordained a bishop at age 50, serving the Manor congregation. He was a church leader of note, he traveled widely, and his services for marriages and funerals were numerous. He was a forceful speaker, devout, generous, and highly respected.

David married Mary Reichard in 1841, a member of the neighboring St. Mark's Episcopal Church. He died at his home near Fairplay on January 23, 1897.

Mary Reichard Long was born March 25, 1819. She

was known in the community as Aunt Mary Long and to the family as "Mother." She was amiable, lovable, trusting, affectionate, and devoted to her family and her church. Many were her labors of love, with a self-sacrificing spirit. She died August 4, 1890, leaving 11 living children.

Ella Long Remley was born in 1843 and married John Remley from Greencastle, Pennsylvania, on November 23, 1867. He was a teacher at Antietam, Spring Grove, Williamsport, and Hagerstown Academy. He read law and was admitted to the bar in 1876. He was elected states attorney in Washington County. They lived in a fine home on Virginia Avenue in Hagerstown. John died in 1884, leaving mostly debts for Ella to support their seven or eight children under 16 years of age. In 1910 she was listed in the St. Louis, Missouri, census.

Susan Long Yourtee was born July 1, 1844. In 1865 she married Eli Yourtee, of Brownsville, Maryland, who was elected to the ministry in Kansas City in 1871. He was an elder at the Brownsville church. They had seven children. Susan died in 1904 and Eli in 1909.

Daniel Melvin Long was born in July 1846. He was always interested in books and learning. He completed two years at Maryland Normal School. He organized and became principal of Linden Seminary in Hagerstown. He taught at Juniata College and later was principal of public schools in Trappe, Maryland. In 1881 he married Mary Cross. They had 10 children. He died in February 1911.

Mary Francis Long Holsinger was born in May 1848. She married Frank Holsinger on November 23, 1867. Frank was a fruit grower in Bedford County, Pennsylvania, until they moved to Kansas in 1870. They had seven children. Frank wrote a column called Woodbury Kid. In Kansas, Frank started a nursery and greenhouse business, which is still operating. Mary died in 1932, 16 years after Frank's death in 1916.

Annie (Lizzie) Long Kendig was born in March 1850. She was married in January 1875, the second wife of Emanuel Kendig, an elder in the Church of the Brethren. Lizzie raised her niece, Mable Kendig Long Timberlake, and her stepson. She had two sons of her own. She died in October 1919.

Joseph Allen Long was born in May 1853. He married Mary Jane Bucher (sister of Orville's wife) in January 1880. He was a minister for 35 years at First Church of the Brethren, York, Pennsylvania. They had six children. He died November 1927.

Julia Long Shafer was born in December 1855. She became the second wife of Charles Shafer in November 1899 at age 44. She had one stepson but no children of her own. She died in December 1932.

D. Victor Long was born in May 1857. He married Edith Stoner in January 1883. They had three children, all well educated. Ephraim was superintendent of schools in Juniata County, Pennsylvania. Raymond worked for Virginia State Department of Education, and Lula was a professor at University of Maryland and a principal of Boonsboro, Maryland, High School. He was an elder in Manor Church of the Brethren. He owned and operated a canning factory in Boonsboro. He died in 1941.

Orville Long was born in December 1860. He married Millie Bucher, and they had seven children. After she died in 1903, he married Lizzie Lehman, and they had two children. Orville taught high school, farmed, was a fruit grower, and the first pastor of the Roaring Spring Church of the Brethren. He was administrator of Morrison's Cove Home for the Aged in Martinsburg, Pennsylvania. He moved to California in 1914, where he preached and bought an Orange Grove. He died in 1938.

Wilmer Long, Orville's twin, was born in December 1860. He died in March 1862.

Walter S. Long was born in November 1863. He married Alice Coffman in 1886. They had no children. He was elder and minister in Twenty-eighth Street Church of the Brethren in Altoona, Pennsylvania, for many years. He died in May 1953.

The Long homestead and buildings on Jordan Road are still in regular use. The present owners are Tom and Judy Shaw.